FERALS

FERALS

BY JACOB GREY

HARPER

An Imprint of HarperCollins*Publishers*

Library of Congress Control Number: 2014952522
ISBN 978-0-06-232103-9 (trade bdg.)

Typography by Sarah Creech
15 16 17 18 19   CG/RRDH   10 9 8 7 6 5 4 3 2 1

❖

First Edition

With special thanks to Michael Ford

FERALS

Some of the victims were found with tooth marks on their bodies. Others were dropped from great heights or bloated with poisons in their blood. To this day, no one knows what—or who—was behind the strange series of murders that swept through Blackstone that fateful summer.

—THE MYSTERY OF THE DARK SUMMER *by Josephine Wallace, Head Librarian, Blackstone Central Library*

1

The night belonged to him. He wore its shadows, tasted its scents. He savored its sounds and silences. Caw leaped from roof to roof, a boy witnessed only by the white eye of the moon and the three crows that soared in the dark sky above him.

Blackstone sprawled like a bacterial growth on all sides. Caw took in flashes of the city—skyscrapers rising to the east, and to the west, the endless slanting roofs of the poorer districts and the smoking chimneys of the industrial quarter. In the north loomed abandoned tenements. The river Blackwater was somewhere to the south, a roiling sludge carrying filth away from the city but never making it any cleaner. Caw could smell its fetid stench.

He skidded up against the dirty glass panel of a skylight. Laying his hands softly on the glass, Caw peered into its soft glow. A hunched janitor wheeled a mop and bucket through the hallway below, lost in his own world. He didn't look up. They never did.

Caw took off again, startling a fat pigeon and skipping around an ancient billboard, trusting his crows to follow. Two of the birds were barely visible—flitting shadows black as tar. The third was white, his pale feathers making him glow like a ghost in the darkness.

I'm starving, muttered Screech, the smallest of the crows. His voice was a reedy squawk.

You're always starving, said Glum, his wing beats slow and steady. *The young are so greedy.*

Caw smiled. To anyone else, the crows' voices would merely sound like the cries of regular birds. But Caw heard more. Much more.

I'm still growing! said Screech, flapping indignantly.

Shame your brain isn't, Glum cackled.

Milky, the blind old white crow, drifted above them. As usual, he said nothing at all.

Caw slowed to gather his breath, letting the cool air fill his lungs. He took in the sounds of night—the swish of a car across slick pavement, the thump of distant music. Farther away, a siren and a man shouting, his words unclear. Whether his voice was raised in anger or happiness, Caw didn't care. Down there was for the regular people of Blackstone. Up here, among the skyline silhouettes . . . it was for him and his crows.

He passed through the warm blast of an air-conditioning vent, then paused, nostrils flaring.

Food. Something salty.

Caw jogged to the edge of the rooftop and peered over. Down below, a door opened onto an alley filled with Dumpsters. It was the back of a twenty-four-hour restaurant. Caw knew they often threw out perfectly good food—leftovers, probably, but he wasn't fussy. He let his glance flick into every dark corner. He saw nothing that worried him, but it was always risky at ground level. Their place, not his.

Glum landed next to Caw and cocked his head. His stubby beak glinted gold, reflecting a streetlight. *You think it's safe?* he asked.

A sudden motion drew Caw's gaze; a rat, rooting in the garbage bags below. It lifted its head and eyed him without fear. "I think so," Caw said. "Stay sharp."

He knew they didn't need the warning. After years of scavenging together, he could trust them better than he could himself.

Caw swung a leg over the lip of the roof and landed softly on the platform of the fire escape. Screech swooped down and perched on the side of a bin, while Glum glided to the corner of the roof, overlooking the main street. Milky dropped onto the fire-escape railing, his talons scratching the metal. All keeping watch.

Caw crept down the steps. He crouched for a moment, eyes on the back door of the restaurant. The smell of food made his stomach rumble violently. *Pizza,* he thought. *Burgers too.*

He fished inside the nearest Dumpster and found a yellow polystyrene box, still warm. He cracked it open. Fries! He shoveled them into his mouth. Greasy, salty, a little burned at the edges. They were good. The acid vinegar caught in his throat, but he didn't care.

He hadn't eaten for two days. He swallowed without chewing and almost choked. Then he crammed more down. One fell from his hand and Screech was there in a second, attacking the scrap with his beak.

A hoarse cry from Glum.

Caw flinched and cowered beside the bin, eyes searching the darkness. His heart jolted as four figures filled the end of the alley.

"Hey!" said the tallest. "Get away from our stash!"

Caw scrambled back, holding the box to his chest. Screech took flight, his wings slapping the air.

The figures stepped closer, and an arc of streetlight caught their faces. Boys, perhaps a couple of years older than him. Homeless, by the looks of their tattered clothes.

"There's enough," said Caw, nodding toward the Dumpster. He felt awkward, talking to other people. It happened so rarely. "Enough for all of us," he repeated.

"No, there's not," said a boy with two rings in his upper lip. He walked ahead of the others with a shoulder-rolling swagger. "There's only enough for *us*. You've been stealing."

Shall we get them? said Screech.

Caw shook his head. It wasn't worth getting injured over a few fries.

"Don't shake your head at me, you filthy little thief!" said the tall one. "You're a liar!"

"Gross—he stinks, too," said a smaller boy, sneering.

Caw felt his face getting hot. He took a step backward.

"Where do you think you're going?" asked the boy with the lip rings. "Why don't you stay awhile?" He stepped up to Caw and shoved him roughly in the chest.

The sudden attack took Caw by surprise and he fell, landing on his back. The box flew from his hands, and fries spilled over the ground. The boys closed in.

"Now he's throwing them on the ground!"

"You gonna pick them up?"

Caw scrambled to his feet. They had him trapped. "You can have them."

"Too late for that," said the leader. He ran his tongue over his lip rings. "Now you gotta pay. How much money you got?"

Caw turned out his pockets, his heart thumping. "None."

The glint of a blade, emerging from the boy's pocket. "In that case, we'll take your thieving fingers instead."

The boy lunged forward. Caw grabbed the edge of the Dumpster and vaulted on top of it.

"He's quick, isn't he?" said the boy. "Get him."

The other three surrounded the bin. One swiped at Caw's ankle. Another started to shake the Dumpster. Caw staggered, desperate to keep his balance. They were all laughing.

Caw saw a drainpipe ten feet to his left and jumped. But as

his fingers caught the metal, the piping broke from the wall with a burst of brick dust. He fell and hit the ground on his side, the air exploding from his lungs. Four grinning faces closed in.

"Hold him down!" said the leader.

"Please . . . no . . ." Caw struggled, but the boys sat on his legs and pulled at his arms. He was spread-eagled as the one with the knife loomed over him. "Which will it be, boys?" He pointed the tip of the blade at Caw's hands in turn. "Left or right?"

Caw couldn't see his crows. Fear pumped through his veins.

The boy crouched down, resting his knee on Caw's chest. "Eenie, meenie, miney, mo." The knife's tip danced from side to side.

Watch out, Caw! called Glum. The boys all looked up at the crow's piercing cry. Then a hand reached down from above and gripped the knife wielder by the back of his collar. The boy yelped as he was jerked away from Caw.

There was a cracking sound—skin against skin—and the knife clattered to the ground.

Where'd he come from? said Screech.

Caw sat up. A tall, thin man was holding the boy with the lip rings by the back of his neck. Brown, wiry hair protruded from beneath the man's stained hat. He was wearing several layers of dirty clothing, including an old brown trench coat fastened around his waist with a belt of frayed blue cord. A tufty beard coated his jawline in uneven patches. Caw guessed he was in his midtwenties, and homeless.

"Leave him be," said the man, his voice rasping. In the semidarkness, his mouth was a black hole.

"What's it to you?" said the boy holding Caw's left arm.

The man shoved the boy with the lip rings hard at the Dumpster.

"This guy's crazy!" said the boy holding Caw's legs. "Let's go."

Their leader picked up his knife and brandished it at the homeless man.

"Lucky you're so filthy," he snarled. "Don't want to get my knife dirty. Come on, fellas." The four attackers turned and tore out of the alley.

Caw scrambled to his feet, his breath coming hard. Looking up, he saw his crows perched together on the fire-escape railing, watching silently.

After the gang had rounded the corner, another smaller shape slipped from the alley's darkness to stand close beside the man. It was a boy of about seven or eight, Caw guessed. His narrow face was pale, and his dirty-blond hair stood on end. "Yeah, and don't come back!" he shouted, shaking a fist.

Caw darted toward the fries scattered on the ground. He started dropping them back into the box. No need to waste a good meal. All the while, he felt the gaze of his rescuer and the boy on his back.

When he'd finished, he stuffed the box inside the deep pocket of his coat and hurried to the fire escape.

"Wait," said the man. "Who are you?"

Caw turned to face him but kept his eyes on the ground. "I'm no one."

The man snorted. "Really? So where are your parents, No One?"

Caw shook his head again. He didn't know what else to say.

"You should be careful," said the man.

"I can take care of myself."

"Doesn't look like that to us," said the boy, tilting his chin upward.

Caw heard the crows' claws shifting on the railing above him. The man's eyes flicked up to them and narrowed. His lips turned in the ghost of a smile. "Friends of yours?" he asked.

Time to go home, said Glum.

Caw started up the steel ladder without looking back. He climbed quickly, hand over hand, his nimble feet barely making a sound on the fire escape. When he reached the roof, he took one last glance and saw the man watching him as the young boy rooted in the Dumpster.

"Something bad's coming," called the man. "Something really bad. You get into trouble, talk to the pigeons."

Talk to the pigeons? Caw only talked to crows.

Pigeons! Screech said, as if he'd heard Caw's thought. *You'd get more sense out of a rock!*

Probably off his rocker, said Glum. *A lot of humans are.*

8

Caw heaved himself onto the roof and set off at a jog. But as he ran, he couldn't shake the man's parting words. He hadn't seemed crazy at all. His face was fierce, his eyes clear. Not like the old drunks who stumbled around the streets or squatted in doorways begging for money.

And, more than that, he had helped Caw. He'd put himself at risk, for no reason.

Caw's crows flew above him, wheeling around buildings and circling back as they made their way to the safety of the nest. Home.

His heart began to slow as the night took him into its dark embrace.

2

It's the same dream. The same as always.

He's back at his old house. The bed is so soft he feels like he's lying on a cloud. It's warm too, and he longs to turn over, pull the duvet tight to his chin, and fall back asleep. But he never can. Because the dream isn't just a dream. It's a memory.

Hurried footsteps on the stairs outside his room. They're coming for him.

He swings his legs out, and his toes sink into the thick carpet. His bedroom is in shadow, but he can just make out his toys lining the top of a chest of drawers and a shelf stacked with picture books.

A crack of light appears under his door and he hears his parents' voices, urgent and hushed.

The door handle turns, and they enter. His mother is wearing a black dress, and her cheeks are silver with tears. His father is dressed in brown corduroy trousers and a shirt open at the neck. His forehead is sweaty.

"Please, no . . . ," Caw says.

His mother takes his hand in hers, her palms clammy, and pulls him toward the window.

Caw tries to tug back, but he's young in the dream, and she's too strong for him.

"Don't fight," she says. "Please. It's for the best. I promise."

Caw kicks her in the shins and scratches at her with his nails, but she gathers him close to her body in a grip of iron and bundles him to the window ledge. Terrified, Caw fastens his teeth on her forearm. She doesn't let go, even when his teeth break her skin. His father draws back the curtains, and for a second Caw catches sight of his own face in the black shine of the window—pudgy, wide-eyed, afraid.

The window is flung open, and the cold night air rushes in.

Now his father holds him as well—his parents have an arm and a leg each. Caw bucks and writhes, screaming.

"Hush! Hush!" says his mother. "It's all right."

The end of the nightmare is coming, but knowing that doesn't make it any less terrible. They push and pull him over the ledge, so his legs are dangling, and he sees the ground far below. His father's jaw is taut, brutal. He won't look Caw in the eye. But Caw can see that he's crying too.

"Do it!" says his father, releasing his grip. "Just do it!"

Why? Caw wants to shout. But all that comes out is a child's wailing cry.

"I'm sorry," says his mother. That's when she shoves him out of the window.

For a split second, his stomach turns. But then the crows have him.

11

They cover his arms and legs, talons digging into his skin and pajamas. A dark cloud that appears out of nowhere, carrying him upward.

His face is filled with feathers and their earthy smell.

He's floating, up and up, carried beneath their black eyes and brittle legs and snapping wings.

He gives his body to the birds and the rhythm of their flight, prepares to wake. . . .

But tonight, he does not.

The crows descend and set him down lightly on the pavement, looping back toward his house along a pale driveway running between tall trees. He sees his parents at his window, now closed. They're hugging, holding each other.

How could they?

Still, he does not wake.

Then Caw sees a figure, a thing, *materializing from the darkness of the front garden, taking slow, deliberate strides to the door of the house. It's tall, almost as tall as the doorway itself, and very thin, with spindly limbs too long for its body.*

The dream has never continued like this before. This is no longer part of his memory—somehow Caw knows that, deep in his bones.

By some trick, he can see the thing's face, close up. It's a man—but the likes of which he's never seen. He wants to look away, but his eyes are drawn to the pale features, made paler still by the blackness of the man's hair, which sits in jagged spikes over his forehead and one eye. He would be handsome if it weren't for his eyes. They're completely black—all pupil, no white.

Caw has no idea who the man is, but he knows that he is more than just bad. The man's slender body draws the darkness to him. He has come here to do harm. Evil. The word comes unbidden. Caw wants to shout, but he is voiceless with fear.

He is desperate to wake, but he does not.

The visitor's lips twist into a smile as he lifts a hand, the fingers like drooping arachnid legs. Caw sees that he's wearing a large golden ring as his fingers enfold the door knocker, like a flower's petals closing. And now the ring is all he sees, and the picture inscribed on its oval surface. A spider carved in sharp lines, eight legs bristling. Its body is a looping single line, with a small curve for the head and a larger one for the body. On its back, a shape that looks like the letter M.

The stranger knocks a single time, then turns his head. He's looking right at Caw. For a moment the crows are gone, and there is nothing in the world but Caw and the stranger. The man's voice whispers softly, his lips barely moving.

"I'm coming for you."

Caw woke up screaming.

Sweat was drying on his forehead, and goose pimples covered his arms. He could see his breath, even under the cover of the tarpaulin that stretched between the branches overhead. As he sat up, the tree creaked and the nest rocked slightly. A spider scuttled away from his hand.

A coincidence. Just a coincidence.

What's up? said Screech, flapping across from the nest's edge to land beside him.

Caw closed his eyes, and the image of the spider ring burned behind his lids.

"Just the dream," he said. "The usual one. Go back to sleep."

Except tonight it *hadn't* been. The stranger—the man at the door—that hadn't really happened. Had it?

We were trying to sleep, said Glum. *But you woke us twitching like a half-eaten worm. Even poor old Milky's up.* Caw could hear the grumpy ruffle of Glum's feathers.

"Sorry," he said. He lay back down, but sleep wouldn't come, not with the dream throwing its fading echoes through his mind. After years of the same nightmare, why had tonight been different?

Caw threw off his blanket and let his eyes adjust to the gloom. The nest was a platform high up in a tree, ten feet across, made of scrap timber and woven branches, with a hatch in the floor he'd made using a sheet of corrugated semitransparent plastic. More branches were knitted together around the nest's edge, with pieces of boarding he'd scavenged from a building site, making a bowl shape with steep sides about three feet tall. His few possessions lay in a battered suitcase he'd found on the banks of the Blackwater several months ago. An old curtain could be pinned across the middle if he wanted privacy from the crows, though Glum never quite got the hint. At the far end, a small hole in the tarpaulin roof offered an entrance and exit for the crows.

It was cold up here, especially in winter, but it was dry.

When the crows had first brought him to the old park eight years ago, they'd settled in an abandoned tree house in a lower fork of the tree. But as soon as he was old enough to climb, Caw had built his own nest up here, hidden away from the world. He was proud of it. It was home.

Caw unhooked the edge of the tarpaulin and pulled it aside. A drop of rainwater splashed onto the back of his neck, and he shuddered.

The moon over the park was a small sliver short of full in a cloudless sky. Milky perched on the branch outside, motionless, his white feathers silver in the moonlight. His head swiveled and a pale, sightless eye seemed to pick Caw out.

So much for sleep, grumbled Glum, shaking his beak disapprovingly.

Screech hopped onto Caw's arm and blinked twice. *Don't mind Glum,* he said. *Old-timers like him need their beauty sleep.*

Glum gave a harsh squawk. *Keep your beak shut, Screech.*

Caw breathed in the smells of the city. Car fumes. Mold. Something dying in a gutter. It had been raining, but no amount of rain could make Blackstone smell clean.

His stomach growled, but he was glad of his hunger. It sharpened his senses, pushed back the terror into the shadows of his mind. He needed air. He needed to clear his head. "I'm going to find something to eat."

Now? said Glum. *You ate yesterday.*

Caw spotted last night's fries container on the far side of the nest, along with the other rubbish the crows liked to collect. Glittering stuff. Bottle tops, cans, ring pulls, foil. The remains of Glum's dinner were scattered about too—a few mouse bones, picked clean. A tiny broken skull.

I could eat too, said Screech, stretching his wings.

Like I always say, said Glum with a shake of his beak. *Greedy.*

"Don't worry," Caw told them. "I'll be back soon."

He opened the hatch, swung out from the platform and into the upper branches, then picked his way down by handholds he could have found with his eyes shut. As he dropped to the ground, three shapes—two black, one white—swooped onto the grass.

Caw felt a little stab of annoyance. "I don't need you to come," he said, for what seemed like the thousandth time. *I'm not a little kid anymore,* he almost added, but he knew that would make him sound even more like one.

Humor us, said Glum.

Caw shrugged.

The park gates hadn't been opened for years, so the place was empty as always. Quiet too, but for the whisper of wind in the leaves. Still, Caw stuck to the shadows. The sole of his left shoe flapped open. He'd need to steal a new pair soon.

He passed the rusty jungle gym where children never played, crossed the flower beds that had long ago given way to weeds. The surface of the fishpond was thick with scum. Screech had sworn he saw a fish in there a month ago, but Glum said he was making it up. Blackstone Prison loomed beyond the park walls on the left, its four towers piercing the sky. On some nights Caw heard sounds from inside, muted by the thick, windowless walls.

As Caw paused by the empty bandstand, covered in graffiti scrawls, Screech landed on the step, talons tip-tapping on the concrete.

Something's wrong, isn't it? he asked.

Caw rolled his eyes. "You don't give up, do you?"

Screech cocked his head.

"It was my dream," Caw admitted. "It wasn't quite the same. I don't understand."

The nightmare forced its way into his mind again. The man with the black eyes. His shadow falling across the ground like a shard of midnight. The hand reaching out, and the spider ring . . .

Your parents belong in the past, said Screech. *Forget them.*

Caw nodded, feeling the familiar ache in his chest. Every time he thought of them, the pain was like a bruise, freshly touched. He would never forget. Each night he relived it. The empty air beneath his wheeling feet; the crack and flap of the crows' wings above.

Since then many crows had come and gone. Sharpy. Pluck. One-legged Dover. Inkspot, with her taste for coffee. Only one crow had remained at his side since that night eight years ago—mute, blind, white-feathered Milky. Glum had been a nest-mate for five years, Screech for three. One with nothing useful to say, one with nothing cheerful, and one with nothing to say at all.

Caw scaled the wrought-iron gates, gripped the looping *B* of *Blackstone Park*, and hauled himself onto the wall. He balanced easily, his hands stuffed casually in his pockets as he walked along the top of it. For Caw, it was almost as easy as walking down the street. He could see Milky and Glum circling high overhead.

I thought we were getting food, said Screech.

"Soon," Caw told him.

He stopped opposite the prison. An ancient beech tree overhung the wall, and he was almost hidden by its thick leaves.

Not here again! squawked Glum, making a branch quiver as he landed.

"Humor me," said Caw pointedly.

He stared at the grand house across the road, built in the shadow of the prison.

Caw often came to look at the house. He couldn't really explain why. Perhaps it was seeing a normal family doing normal things. Caw liked to watch them eating dinner together, or playing board games, or just sitting in front of their TV.

The crows had never understood.

A shadow in the garden snatched him suddenly back to his nightmare. The stranger's cruel smile. The spider hand. The weird ring. Caw focused intently on the house, trying to drive the terrifying images away.

He wasn't sure what time it was, but the windows of the house were dark, the curtains drawn. Caw rarely saw the mother, but he knew that the father worked at the prison. Caw had seen him leaving the prison gates and returning home. He always wore a suit, so Caw guessed he was more than just a guard. His black car squatted in the driveway like a sleeping animal. The girl with the red hair, she'd be in bed, her little dog lying at her feet. She was about his age, Caw guessed.

AWOOOOOOOOO!

A wailing sound cut through the night, making Caw jerk up. He dropped into a crouch on the wall, gripping the stone as the siren rose and fell, shockingly loud in the moonlit silence.

From the four towers of the prison, floodlights flashed on, throwing arcs of white light into the prison and on the road outside. Caw shrank back, sheltering under the branches, away from the glare.

Let's scram, said Screech, twitching his feathers nervously. *There'll be humans here soon.*

"Wait," said Caw, holding up a hand.

A light blinked on in the upstairs room where the girl's parents slept.

For once I agree with Screech, said Glum.

"Not yet."

More lights came on behind closed curtains, and a minute or two later, the front door opened. Caw trusted the darkness to shield him. He watched as the girl's father stepped out. He was a slender but tough-looking man, with fair hair receding a little at the front. He was straightening a tie and speaking into a phone clamped against his shoulder.

It's the one who walks that horrible dog! Glum said, hissing with disgust. Caw strained his ears to hear the man's voice over the siren.

"I'll be there in three minutes," shouted the man. "I want complete lockdown, a timeline, and a map of the sewers." A pause. "I don't care whose fault it was. Meet me out front with everyone you can spare." Another pause. "Yes, of *course* you should call the police commissioner! She needs to know about this, and fast. Get on it now!"

He slipped the phone away and strode fast toward the prison.

"What's going on?" Caw muttered.

Who cares? said Screech. *Human stuff. Let's go.*

As Caw watched, the girl appeared in the doorway of the house with the dog at her heels. She was wearing a green dressing gown. Her face was delicate, almost a perfect inverted triangle, with wide-set eyes and a small, pointed chin. Her red hair, the same color as her mother's, hung loose and messy to her shoulders. "Dad?" she said.

"Stay inside, Lydia," snapped the man, barely looking back.

Caw gripped the wall tighter.

Her father broke into a trot down the pavement.

The spider this way crawls, said a voice, close to Caw's ear.

Caw flinched. He glanced up and saw Milky perched on a branch. Glum snapped his head around.

Did you just . . . speak? he said.

Milky blinked, and Caw stared into the pale film of the old crow's eyes. "Milky?" he said.

The spider this way crawls, said the white crow, again. His voice was like the rasp of wind over dried leaves. *And we are but prey in his web.*

I told you the old snowball's bonkers, cackled Screech.

Caw's throat had gone dry. "What do you mean, *the spider*?" he asked.

Milky stared back at him. Lydia was still at the door, watching.

"What spider, Milky?" Caw said again.

But the white crow was silent.

Something was happening. Something big. And whatever it was, Caw wasn't going to miss it.

"Come on," he said at last. "We're following that man."

3

Caw tiptoed along the top of the park wall, keeping pace with Lydia's father.

This is ridiculous, said Glum. *You'll get us into trouble again, just like last night.*

Caw ignored him. They reached the end of the wall, and the man took a right turn toward the prison gates. For a moment Caw panicked. He couldn't follow without being seen. But then he remembered.

"Meet me on the roof," he said to the crows, then slipped down and ran across the dark, deserted road. On the far side, an abandoned building stood on the corner of the street, half-demolished, with one wall completely gone, the insides exposed to the elements. Caw could see skeletal hulks of old machines within. Whatever they used to make, their days of usefulness were a long-forgotten memory.

Caw scrambled over the rubble up to the second floor, careful not to make a sound. He skirted boxes piled high with old books, their covers mostly rotted away. He climbed two flights of stairs toward a hatch that opened onto a roof of corrugated metal. Then he crept to the highest point, where Glum, Screech, and Milky were already perched, just as Lydia's father reached the prison far below on the opposite side of the street.

A dozen men and women in prison guard uniform were standing in groups just outside the open gates, illuminated by the floodlights, looking nervous but excited. Dogs strained at their leads, nosing the air.

The wailing siren cut out suddenly, and the vibrations faded on the air.

"Where's that plan of the sewers?" said Lydia's father. His voice carried clearly up to Caw.

One of the men laid a large sheet of paper on the hood of a car parked by the sidewalk.

Caw's heart quickened. He was right to think that Lydia's father wasn't just a guard. He was ordering the others around like he was in charge of the whole prison!

"The police will be here in the next five minutes, but we can't afford to wait. The clock is ticking. Everyone get into pairs. One dog per pair. Fan out into the surrounding streets. Check every manhole cover. If you see them, call it in. Don't try to apprehend them—you know who we're dealing with. And be careful!"

The guards started to disperse, while Lydia's father peered at the map. Within moments, he was alone.

Can we please go home now? said Glum, fluffing out his feathers. *It's freezing!*

Hey, over here! called Screech.

Caw turned around—the youngest of the crows was perched at the other end of the roof. A faint grinding sound was rising up from below. *Something's happening down there,* said Screech.

Caw looked at Lydia's father. His head had jerked up, as though he'd heard it too. He swiftly folded the map and began to pace across the street.

Caw ran over the roof to join Screech and stared down into an alley that ran between the building he was perched on and a derelict warehouse beyond.

The alley was empty, apart from a few strewn papers and some Dumpster bins. One end forked into a maze of passages running between more abandoned buildings—the other made its way to the main street that ran beside the park.

With another grinding sound, the manhole cover directly below Caw turned. One side cracked open, then the whole thing lifted free and was tossed aside like it weighed nothing, spinning like a coin, then settling flat. Caw shrank back, peering over the roof's parapet. Something small scurried out of the dark hole in the ground. An insect, or maybe a spider. And then two hands emerged. Big, meaty hands. A huge figure heaved itself into the open. Caw saw a bald head, a great gleaming dome of skin stretched

25

over skull. The man wore an orange shirt and trousers.

Suddenly it made sense. The guards in a panic. The search parties.

"An escaped prisoner," Caw whispered. "That's who they're looking for!"

I can see that, said Glum.

The man tipped back his head, and terror caught in Caw's throat. Something was wrong with the man's mouth. It was too wide, like his cheeks were split in a hideous grin. Then, after a heartbeat, Caw realized it was a tattoo. A permanent smile.

He's a looker, Screech muttered.

The prisoner started to tear off his shirt and called down into the manhole in a muted voice, "All clear!" Then the man tossed the ripped prison shirt aside and turned back around.

As Caw saw the man's bare chest, he felt his bones turn to ice. A new wave of terror hit him, deeper than anything he'd felt outside his nightmares. Pure fear, straight from the darkest depths of his mind, undimmed by logic and impossible to ignore. It squeezed each of his nerve endings and turned his stomach to water.

Inked across the massive man's chest was a tattoo that rippled with his muscles, almost as though it was alive. Eight legs, scurrying.

A spider.

And not just any spider. Its body was a looping line, and a spiky M shape was emblazoned inside it.

Caw gripped the parapet, his mouth dry as dust.

It was the spider from his dream.

Beside him, Milky ruffled his feathers.

The tattooed prisoner leaned over the manhole, took hold of a skinny wrist, and pulled a second figure into the open—a young woman. She had black hair that fell to her waist and caught the streetlight like a raven's wing. As she straightened up, she stood even taller than the man. The sleeves of her prison uniform were soiled with dirty water from the sewer, and she began carefully rolling them up. Her arms were lithe and muscled, as though she could wrap them around a person and squeeze their life away.

And then came a third person. He flopped out into the alley and scrambled to his feet, brushing down his clothes. He was less than half the height of the others and hunched over. He looked old, but he moved like a younger man, feet turning this way and that. His eyes darted around in all directions.

"Finally, the smells of the city!" said the short man. "How I missed the delicious stench of rot."

The big man cracked his knuckles. "Time to get back to business," he said.

"We shouldn't delay," hissed the woman. Her voice was soft and sibilant. "It won't be long before they work out where that tunnel leads."

"Freeze!"

All three prisoners turned to the far end of the alley. A man stood silhouetted there, holding a gun, its barrel glinting.

Oh dear, Glum said.

It was the man from the house. But the prisoners didn't look afraid. Instead, the big one stepped forward.

"Warden Strickham," he said. "What a *nice* surprise."

We should go, said Glum. *This has nothing to do with us. It's—*

"Human stuff?" whispered Caw. "I know. But in case you hadn't noticed, I am a human, Glum."

That wasn't why he was staying, though. He didn't want to say it out loud, but he needed to know about that tattoo. He had to find out what it meant.

"You're going right back to jail, Jawbone," said Mr. Strickham.

The big man, Jawbone, grinned for real. It twisted his face, making him look even scarier, like a hungry dog. "What d'you say, friends? Should we crawl back to our cells?"

The short man sniggered, and the woman's tongue flickered over her lips. "I say we refuse his kind offer," she said. "He tastes a little *scared* to me."

Mr. Strickham brought his other hand to the hilt of his gun to steady it. "I don't think so," he said. "I'm the one with the bullets. And a squad of police officers on the way." He glanced behind him.

Suddenly Caw felt nervous.

"Leave this to me," said Jawbone. "I'll catch up when I've dealt with him."

The others nodded and melted away into the alley—the short man shuffling, his tall companion almost gliding.

"Hey!" shouted Mr. Strickham. "One more move and I'll shoot!"

There was a flash and a deafening crack as Mr. Strickham's pistol went off. A warning shot, but the prisoners ignored it. The woman took one fork, the short man the other. The next moment they were gone.

"Just us now," said Jawbone, moving slowly toward Mr. Strickham.

"I don't like this," said Caw. "We should help him."

In a flash, Jawbone lunged, and his shovel-like hand gripped the gun and twisted it from the warden's hand. With a cry of pain, Mr. Strickham cradled his arm, backing away.

Jawbone tossed the gun behind him. "Never liked guns," he said. "They kill too quick." He reached out and gripped Mr. Strickham's neck, then hoisted him one-handed into the air. The warden's legs kicked out weakly as his face turned red, then purple.

Caw's stomach churned with fear. It was a long way down from where he stood on the roof. He thought he could make it with a couple of jumps, but what then? He swallowed and swung a leg over the parapet.

Then a new voice called out, "Leave him alone!"

At the end of the alley, a small shape had slipped from the shadows. Caw caught his breath. It was Lydia—the girl from the house! She still wore her pajamas and a dressing gown. One of the laces of her sneakers was trailing. How had Caw not seen her follow him?

Her father twitched in Jawbone's death grip, his face horribly contorted. Jawbone grinned, then threw him aside like a rag doll. Mr. Strickham slammed into a Dumpster and collapsed in a heap.

"Lydia?" he croaked, managing to get to one knee. "Oh, God. No."

Jawbone aimed a kick at Mr. Strickham's stomach, and he crumpled with a moan.

"Dad!" shouted Lydia, rushing toward him. Jawbone grabbed at her, seizing a handful of her hair and yanking her around. Her face twisted in pain.

"Let me go!" she yelled, scrabbling at his arm.

"Now!" whispered Caw to the crows. "Get him!"

He swung his other leg over the parapet, then pushed off and plummeted, hitting the ground hard. He fell into a backward roll, coming up to see that Screech and Glum had already swooped down onto Jawbone's head. *Kow-kow-kow!* they screamed.

Jawbone dropped Lydia and swatted at the crows with his massive arms.

"Get them off me!" he bellowed.

The prisoner punched the air as the crows raked his face with their claws. A fist caught Screech and sent him crashing into a wall. He slid to the ground but flapped away just as Jawbone's foot came down in a stamp. Glum squawked and stabbed his beak at the prisoner's eyes. Jawbone staggered, his spider tattoo writhing as he fought off the attack. Screech threw himself bravely back into the fray.

Caw rushed to Mr. Strickham's side, and he and Lydia helped him stand. At the same time Caw realized that the girl was staring at him, openmouthed.

Mr. Strickham frowned in confusion, watching the crows swirl around Jawbone in a blur of feathers. The giant was twisting like a man fighting shadows.

"Come on!" Caw said, pulling Mr. Strickham away. "Run!"

But Mr. Strickham staggered in the opposite direction, and Caw saw he was heading for the gun on the ground.

"Dad! Leave it!" said Lydia, running after him. Too late. Mr. Strickham had reached the gun. He wheeled around, bringing the barrel up to point at Jawbone. And the crows.

"No!" yelled Caw. He threw himself at the warden's arm as the gun went off with a crack. The sound rang through his ears, and Caw clenched his eyes shut against the stabbing pain. When he opened them again, Mr. Strickham was mouthing at him furiously, but Caw couldn't hear the words. He turned and saw that Jawbone had gone, and so had his crows.

Gradually sound seeped through his eardrums.

". . . saved us, Dad," Lydia was saying.

"He helped him escape!" said Mr. Strickham.

Lydia put a hand on his arm. "That man was going to kill you!"

The radio on Mr. Strickham's belt crackled, and panicked voices came through. *"Sir, where are you? . . . Shots fired! . . . Warden Strickham?"*

Mr. Strickham plucked the radio off his hip. "Alleyway between Rector and Fourth," he said. "I've lost them."

The hard lines of Mr. Strickham's face softened. He looked at Caw, and his nostrils twitched like he'd smelled something bad. Lydia was looking at Caw too, and he felt his face getting hot. "Who are you?" said Mr. Strickham.

Caw didn't know what to say. If there were police on the way, he had to leave, or they'd send him to an orphanage. His eyes searched the roofline for the crows.

"Those birds," said the warden. "What *was* that?"

Caw backed away, letting his feet take him toward the other end of the alley. He felt trapped. The crows were right—he should never have interfered.

"Hey! You're not going anywhere, young man!" said Mr.

Strickham. "I need a statement."

Caw turned and ran. His ears picked up the sound of dogs barking again, not far off. He heard another crackle of a radio. He had to get back to the nest.

"Come back!" said Mr. Strickham.

"At least tell us your name!" Lydia shouted after him.

Caw reached the street and saw cops running toward him.

Up here! Screech called.

Caw glanced up and saw the three crows perched on a chain-link fence sixty feet away, where the street ran to a dead end. One of Screech's legs looked crooked, as though it was broken. *He's hurt,* thought Caw. *He's hurt because of me.*

There was a patch of waste ground beyond. The old railway station. Caw ran toward the fence.

Flashlight beams picked out his body, and several voices yelled at him to stop.

He leaped onto the metal mesh and swung his legs over the top, landing on the other side. When he looked back, he saw a dozen officers coming toward him, with three or four dogs. Lydia and her father were there too.

Caw slid down an embankment just beyond the fence, out of sight.

"Hold it!" cried the warden.

No way, thought Caw. He ran, and he didn't stop until he'd doubled back to reach the park again. He peered at both ends of the street, making sure that no one was watching, then climbed over the gate. As he scrambled over, one of his flapping shoes came loose and fell to the street. No time to go back for it. He jumped down to the other side.

Finally, his pumping blood began to calm. He was safe here in the shadows. Home.

He walked slowly back to his tree, limping a little on one bare foot.

Well, that was fun! said Glum sarcastically, already in the nest as Caw clambered up.

Did you see me? said Screech. *The way I got him?* He spread his wings, mimicking his actions. *Peck! Scratch! Claw!*

Caw heaved himself onto his bed and lay on his back, letting the sweat cool on his body. He suddenly felt very tired indeed.

I was pretty brave, right? said Screech.

"You were both incredible," Caw told them.

Milky was perched at the side of the nest, looking completely unruffled. He hadn't joined in the fighting. His blind eyes stared in Caw's direction.

"What's going on, Milky?" asked Caw. "Who were those prisoners?"

The old white crow was silent and still as a marble statue.

I think he's done talking, said Glum.

"The spider," said Caw. "I dreamed it. And then it was there in real life, on that prisoner's chest. You know what it means, don't you?"

Milky cocked his head and turned away.

4

Caw woke to the crows all squawking as one. The nest was rocking gently.

"What's going on?" he said.

Get away! yelped Screech, flapping madly. *Intruder!*

Adrenaline flooded through Caw's body and he sat up, reaching for a weapon. He managed to find a bent plastic spoon, just in time to see a head poking up through the hatch.

"Wow!" said Lydia, resting her hands on the timbers of the nest. "This place is amazing! It's way bigger than it looks from down there."

Caw pressed himself into a corner, clutching the spoon in front of him like a knife. She was wearing a baseball cap, which made her red hair fall straight, curling under her chin. In the light of day, he realized she had a smattering of freckles he hadn't seen the night before. Her eyes shone.

"Hey! Don't point that thing at me!" she said.

"How did you find me?" Caw demanded. "No one knows about this place!"

Lydia beamed with pride. "I'm good at sniffing things out," she said. "I've seen you sneaking around by our place before, watching us from the wall next to our house. So I figured you must live around here somewhere. And when I was out walking Benjy this morning, I found this by the park gate."

Lydia dropped Caw's shoe on the floor of the nest.

"I figured the park would be a perfect place to go if you didn't want to be found. So I hopped over the gate and searched until I saw this funny thing stuck up in a tree. Not bad, huh?"

Suddenly Caw felt silly. But he was too embarrassed to lower the spoon.

"What are you doing here?" he said.

Lydia smiled. "I could ask you the same question. Don't you have a home? Don't you have parents?"

Caw shrugged. "I live here," he said. "Just me."

"Cool!" she said. "Are you going to invite me in?"

Caw glanced at Glum. *Don't even think about it,* said the crow, puffing out his chest.

"No," said Caw.

"Oh, come on!" she said. "Pretty please?"

Give her a little shove, said Screech. The young crow hopped forward menacingly, then skipped back again.

"No!" said Caw. "Leave me alone!"

The girl's face fell. "All right, all right," she said. "Chill out. Just give me a second to catch my breath, okay? Then I'll go."

As she tucked a lock of hair back into her cap, still with just her head and shoulders poking into the nest, Caw's fear evaporated. She was just a girl. What harm could she do?

Lydia blew out her cheeks. "Okay. I'll go," she said.

"Wait!" said Caw. He glanced at the crows, then sighed. "You can come in for a bit," he mumbled.

No! said the crows in unison. Caw lowered the spoon.

"Phew!" she said, grinning. "You could really have hurt me with that."

Despite himself, Caw couldn't help smiling.

Lydia scrambled up into the nest and settled cross-legged on the platform. She was wearing jeans and a pale hooded top, streaked with leaves and dirt. She took off her cap and shook her hair free, watching Screech and Glum with a look of puzzlement. Milky would be outside, Caw knew—he never slept in the nest.

"So these birds are your pets?" she said.

I am not a pet! said Glum.

And I'm not just any bird! protested Screech. *I'm a crow.*

"Sort of," said Caw.

Sort of? said Glum and Screech together. Lydia jerked back a little. Caw realized that to her it sounded like two angry squawks.

"They live with me," he said.

"Did you train them?"

38

Screech chuckled. *Cha-cha-cha.*

"So, what's it like, hiding out in this park all the time?" Lydia asked.

Caw felt a flash of annoyance. "I'm not hiding," he said.

"Okay, then. So why are you always spying on me?"

Caw couldn't hold her stare. "I wasn't."

"Liar," she said, but with a smile. "I thought you were a burglar at first, but then I thought, no one's stupid enough to rob the warden of Blackstone Prison. Anyway, I forgive you. I'm Lydia, by the way." She held out her hand.

Caw looked at it.

She leaned forward and took his hand, placing it in hers, then shook it up and down. "And you are?"

"I'm . . . Caw," said Caw.

Lydia grinned. "What sort of a name is that?"

Caw shrugged. "It's what I'm called."

"If you say so." Lydia looked around the nest. "So, did you build this place?"

Caw nodded. He couldn't help a flush of pride.

With some help! said Screech.

Lydia looked up, narrowing her eyes at the crows.

"With some help," Caw added.

"Are you talking to the birds?"

Crows, please, said Glum.

"Well . . . ," said Caw. He almost lied, then thought better of it. "Yes. And they're crows."

"Okay, that's seriously weird," said Lydia.

Glum hissed at her.

"Sorry," she said nervously.

"Don't worry," said Caw. "He's always in a bad mood."

Take that back! said Glum.

Lydia cocked her head. "I just wanted to come and thank you," she said. "You ran away pretty quickly last night."

Caw shrugged. "I just . . . happened to be there. It's no big deal."

"And your crows," said Lydia. "I suppose I should thank them too. They were very brave." She turned to them. "Sorry—*you* were very brave."

Glum ruffled his feathers. *Flattery will get you nowhere, my girl,* he said.

"He says it was nothing," said Caw. Suddenly his stomach let out a rumble. He hadn't eaten a thing since the fries from the restaurant.

Lydia's eyes lit up. "Are you hungry?" she asked, taking off her backpack.

"A little," Caw admitted.

She fished inside and took out a chocolate bar in a blue wrapper. "Here you go," she said, offering it to him across the nest.

Caw took it from her like it was a precious thing and peeled the wrapper away carefully. He couldn't remember the last time he'd eaten chocolate.

Careful, said Glum. *It might be poisoned.*

Caw rolled his eyes, then took a huge bite. His teeth sank through the thick chocolate, and it melted over his tongue. The bar was gone in seconds, sweetness coating the inside of his mouth.

"A *little* hungry?" said Lydia, still grinning. "Here." She handed him an apple. Caw tried to eat it more slowly, in methodical bites. The fruit's flesh exploded juice into his mouth, and it dribbled over his chin.

Save a bit for us! said Screech.

Caw tossed the core to the two crows, who attacked it with their beaks. He didn't worry about saving any for Milky. The white crow rarely ate.

"The scrawny one looks hurt," said Lydia, pointing to Screech's crooked leg.

Who's she calling scrawny? said Screech.

"Come here, little crow," said Lydia soothingly. "Let me take a look."

She'd better not be talking to me, said Screech, lifting his beak haughtily. *I'm not little.*

Glum gave a throaty laugh.

"He's just a bit nervous," said Caw.

Lydia leaned toward Screech. "I could make a splint," she said.

"You've got plenty of junk here I could use. And I'm good with animals."

Screech hopped away from her.

"Let her try," said Caw. "She might be able to help."

"I've got another apple," said Lydia, taking it out of her bag and handing it to him. "Here."

Caw ate, watching as Lydia fashioned a splint out of twigs and string. Screech extended his leg gingerly, and she fastened the splint into place. Milky, he noticed, had dropped into the nest through the small opening in the tarp at the far end. Caw didn't think Lydia even knew he was there. But the blind crow seemed to be watching them with his sightless eyes.

"Done!" she said, with a clap of her hands. "It's not broken, but he should keep it rested."

Screech peered down at the splint. *It's not a half-bad job!* he said.

"He says 'thank you,'" said Caw. He almost smiled again, but caught himself. What was he doing, letting his guard down, welcoming this girl into his most secret place? What if she told her family about it? What if she told everyone? He cleared his throat.

"Look, thank you for the food, but . . ."

"Are those books?" she said, scrambling across the nest. In the corner, beneath Caw's tattered sweater, was his latest stack.

"Yes," said Caw. "But—"

Lydia took one. "They're picture books!" she said, grinning.

42

Caw really wanted her to go now, but he couldn't think of the right words.

"Why are you reading picture books?" she said. "They're for little kids."

Caw felt his blush deepen.

Lydia's look turned to utter dismay. "Wait—I'm sorry. Did you ever learn to read?"

Caw lowered his gaze and managed a tiny shake of his head.

"Hey, these are library books," said Lydia. "Did you . . . steal them?"

"No!" said Caw, glancing up angrily. "I borrowed them."

"You have a library card?" said Lydia, her eyebrow arching.

"Not exactly," said Caw. "A woman—a librarian—leaves them outside for me."

Lydia put the book down. "I could teach you to read," she said.

Caw didn't know what to say. Why was she being so nice to him?

"I mean, if you want me to," she added awkwardly. "Maybe we could go to the library together—pick something to help you learn."

Caw was about to reply when Milky let out a thin cry. Everyone looked at the white crow.

"Whoa, I didn't see him there," said Lydia, shifting uncomfortably. "Why are his feathers like that?"

"They always have been," said Caw, his eyes fixed on Milky.

"Listen, thanks for the offer with the library, but—"

Milky squawked again.

"Sounds like he wants you to come with me," Lydia said with a grin. She pushed out her bottom lip. "But then, I don't speak bird."

Glum hissed.

"That one's touchy, isn't he?" said Lydia.

Caw was watching Milky. Why was the white crow making such a fuss?

Milky blinked. Did he really want Caw to go with this strange girl? It had been Milky's words about the spider that had convinced Caw to follow Lydia's father the night before. And if he hadn't, he never would have seen the tattoo. The one that matched the ring in his dream.

"Come on," Lydia urged. "What harm can a trip to the library do?"

Of course! If anyone could help him understand what the spider symbol meant, it was the librarian. She had so many books.

"So, what do you say?" said Lydia.

Bad idea, said Glum.

I think she's all right, said Screech, holding up his leg.

Caw looked at both of them, then at Lydia. He'd never had a friend before. And she'd gone through a lot of trouble to find him. Milky had spoken for the first time in all the eight years Caw had known him. Perhaps it was a good sign.

"Before you say no, it's my way of saying thanks for saving us," said Lydia.

Caw watched her face closely, as if her features might betray her thoughts. Was he actually ready to trust another human being after avoiding them for so long?

Perhaps not yet. But if he kept his guard up, and the crows were with him . . .

"Okay," he said. "Just this once."

5

Caw always felt on edge when he went out in the daytime. At night, when he scoured the city for food and supplies, the darkness protected him from prying eyes. It allowed him to move freely through the streets and along rooftops. But down on the ground, under the pale spring sunshine, he felt exposed. Cars gridlocked the streets, and hundreds of people filled the sidewalks and shops. He told himself the people weren't looking *at* him, but it never helped.

This time, though, with Lydia at his side, he almost felt normal. Of course he kept an eye on the sky, to check that Screech and Glum were still with them. Milky had remained behind at the nest.

Blackstone was vast, its streets organized on a grid. Caw couldn't read the names on the signs, but he counted the blocks. That way, he always knew where to find the road that led up to the park. As they walked deeper into the city, buildings loomed up on either side, so tall that the sky was just a strip of gray above. The people who lived at the top must feel like they were in a nest, too, he thought.

Monorail lines threaded over the streets on viaducts or plunged into tunnels that burrowed underground. The stations were scattered through the city, disgorging passengers from the bowels of the earth. Caw had never ventured beneath the streets. The thought of being trapped down there chilled him to the bone.

"My dad's so stressed out," Lydia was saying. "He says his job might be on the line. Those prisoners were in maximum security, but they managed to break through the floor of one of the bathroom stalls."

Caw let Lydia talk the whole way. She was good at talking. He learned she was an only child, that her dog, Benjy, was scared of cats, and that her favorite subject at school was math. He was listening, but everywhere he went, his eyes scanned for an escape route, preferably upward—drainpipes, fire escapes, window ledges with enough room to wrap his fingers around them. He wondered when he would find the right moment to tell Lydia that he'd never actually been *inside* the library before.

They were approaching it now, a huge old-fashioned building with a grass forecourt, broken up by paths and strange metal sculptures. The first time he'd gone there was just over a year ago. At twilight, a storm had swept across Blackstone, and he'd taken shelter from the rain under the grand fluted columns that lined the front of the library. He hadn't even known what was inside, but the lights from a window had tempted him to look closer. As he'd pressed his nose against the glass and seen those huge shelves lined with thousands of books, he'd been mesmerized. They reminded him of being a child back in his bedroom on the nights when his mother would pick a picture book from the shelf and read to him until he fell asleep.

A middle-aged woman had taken him by surprise, appearing at the main doors and asking if he wanted to come inside. She was shorter than him by a head, with black skin and tightly curled black hair turning gray in places. It was the first time a human had spoken to him in months, and if the rain hadn't been falling so hard, he would have run away. As it was, he froze on the spot. The woman had smiled and told him she was called Miss Wallace, and that she was the head librarian. She asked him if he liked books. Caw said nothing, but the woman must have seen a look of longing on his face.

"Wait here," she'd said.

And against all his instincts and the advice of the crows, he had.

When the lady had emerged again, she was clutching a pile of colorful books and a steaming cardboard cup. "You look cold," she'd said.

Caw took a cautious sip. Hot chocolate. He closed his eyes, savoring the taste. It was rich and creamy, filling him up the way rainwater never did. She let him choose the books he liked the most—the ones with the fewest words. Maybe she guessed he couldn't read, but she didn't say so.

"Just bring them back the same time next week," she'd said.

"Leave them by the fire-exit steps at the back of the building if you'd rather not come in."

Caw had nodded and tried to say *thank you*, but he was so nervous he'd ended up mouthing it instead.

The following week he'd returned the books and found another pile waiting for him with another cup of hot chocolate. It was the same the next week, and the one after that. Occasionally Miss Wallace would come out and say hello. Only once had she suggested she could call someone—"to help him"—but Caw had shaken his head so violently that she hadn't repeated the offer.

"What happened to your parents, Caw?"

Lydia's question snapped him back to the present.

"I don't mean to pry," she added. "It's just that most kids without parents go to an orphanage."

"I don't know," said Caw cautiously. "I don't remember."

He couldn't tell her about his dreams. She'd only laugh.

"But . . ." She trailed off. Maybe she could sense that he didn't want to talk about it.

They stopped to cross the road.

Glum squawked, swooping down and landing on the traffic light. *She's nosy, this one,* he said.

The library rose ahead. It looked a lot older than most of the buildings in Blackstone. Lydia strode toward the huge double doors, but Caw paused. Now that he was here, he wasn't so confident.

Could he really just march right through the entrance?

"What are you waiting for?" said Lydia.

We'll stay outside, said Glum, settling on the steps. *Be careful.*

Caw knew he looked foolish, so he steeled himself and climbed the steps. A few pigeons scattered out of the way, and Caw suddenly remembered the homeless man from two nights ago, outside the restaurant.

He was probably mad, like Screech had said.

At the top of the steps, Caw felt an odd prickle on the back of his neck. He had the curious sensation he was being watched, but when he turned, no one was there. Just the windswept grass of the forecourt and a couple of empty benches. He followed Lydia through the door.

It was warm inside, and sweat immediately broke out over his forehead. The silence made him suddenly aware of the sound of his own breathing, and his eyes swept the cavernous room. On the far side, rows of towering shelves held thousands of books, and around the top ran a balcony with more shelves. In front were several desks, where people sat reading and writing quietly. On the left, near the entrance, was a curved table with a computer and lots of stacks of paper, and behind it was the librarian. She was leaning over a notepad with her glasses perched low on her nose, and as she looked up and saw Caw, her face broke into a wide smile.

"Well, hello, you!" she said. Her eyes fell on Lydia, and her eyebrows shot up. "And you've brought a friend, I see."

Caw nodded.

"I'm Lydia Strickham," said Lydia. "Pleased to meet you."

"You can call me Miss Wallace," the librarian said. "Now, what can I do for you two?"

Caw placed his books on the desk. "I . . . Can you . . . ," he mumbled, blushing furiously. He felt like running right back through the door and into the cool air outside. "I need to find a book," he said finally.

Miss Wallace clapped her hands together in pleasure. "Well, it's about time!" she said. "I never knew if you liked the ones I was picking out for you. Now, what is it you're looking for?"

Caw glanced around the huge room. "I want to know about spiders," he said. "Unusual ones," he added as an afterthought.

He could sense Lydia frowning, but for once she didn't say anything.

Miss Wallace just smiled. "Follow me," she said.

Caw trailed after her between the stacks, trying not to catch the eye of any of the other readers. He was sure they were looking at him, in his dirty black coat and ragged shoes. The librarian glanced at the shelves, slowed, then paused halfway down. "You'll find natural history here," she said, gesturing to a section of the shelf. "Let's see." She peered closer, then pulled out a book. "This one is an encyclopedia of spider species," she said, handing it to Caw.

51

"There are a few other books on arthropods too. Spiders are a kind of arthropod, you see? I'll be at the desk if you need anything else."

Caw sat on the floor, glad to be out of sight, and Lydia flopped down beside him. "I thought we were coming so I could teach you to read," she muttered. "But you're thinking about the prisoner, aren't you? The big guy in the alley with the creepy tattoo."

Caw nodded, opening the book. "I recognized it," he said.

"From where?"

"From a dream I had," said Caw. "A dream about my parents."

Lydia cocked her head. "I thought you didn't remember anything about your parents."

Caw sighed. He hardly knew what to tell her. He hardly knew what he really *knew*. "I can't explain," he said. "It *feels* like a memory. Except the last time was different. There was this man . . . an evil man . . . he wore a ring with a picture of that spider."

Lydia frowned, looking puzzled. "The same spider?"

"Exactly the same," said Caw. "Will you help me look?"

They sat side by side, flicking through the images of spiders. None of them looked like the one they'd seen, with its looping body, its long, narrow legs, and the *M* design on its back.

After half an hour, Lydia stood up and stretched. "It's not there," she said. "Let's ask Miss Wallace if she can help."

"Find what you're looking for?" asked the librarian cheerily as they walked up to her desk.

Caw shook his head.

"We're looking for a particular spider," said Lydia. "But none of the books show it."

"Hmm," said Miss Wallace. "Could you draw it?"

"I think so," said Lydia. Miss Wallace handed her a sheet of paper and a pencil. "The body was kind of like an S shape," Lydia murmured as she drew. She captured the shape almost perfectly. Just seeing it again made Caw shudder.

"Don't forget the M in the middle," he said. He took the pencil and made the adjustments.

Miss Wallace squinted at it through her glasses. "Are you sure this is a real spider?" she asked. "I've never seen anything like it."

"I just want to know where it comes from," Caw said. "It's important."

"Well, we get all sorts of experts and academics in the library," said Miss Wallace. "Let me make a few calls. Could you come back tomorrow?"

Caw nodded. "Thank you," he said.

"It's no problem," she said. "Would you like to take some more books out while you're here?"

"Yes, please," said Lydia, before Caw had a chance to reply.

When they left the library, Lydia's bag was full of new books, and most of them had a lot more words than Caw was used to. He didn't care, though. He was still thinking about the spider. If he couldn't find it among all those books, what hope did he have of discovering the truth about his dream?

They found Screech and Glum perched on the steps outside, watching a man sitting on a bench across the street eat a hamburger.

This guy hasn't dropped a single crumb, said Screech bitterly.

Find anything interesting? said Glum.

Caw shook his head. "Let's go."

"Don't be depressed," said Lydia. "Miss Wallace might come up with something."

Caw kicked a stone down the sidewalk. "Maybe. Thanks for helping, anyway."

"I've been thinking," said Lydia. "Could the spider have something to do with a gang? You know—a symbol, rather than a real spider. Were your parents in any sort of trouble?"

Best to forget about it, said Glum, landing ahead of them. *Get back to normal.*

"I don't think so," said Caw. "I don't know." There was a lot he didn't know about them.

They reached the edge of the park at about midday.

"Listen," said Lydia. "I have to go now. But why don't you come to our house for dinner tonight?"

No way! said Screech.

Bad, bad idea, Glum added.

"Erm . . . ," said Caw.

This has gone far enough, Glum cut in. *First this girl sneaks into our nest, and then she drags you halfway across the city, and now this!*

"Come on!" said Lydia. "It's the least we can do after you saved us from those prisoners. Think of it—a hot meal! You look like you could do with one."

We don't need her, said Screech, flapping. Caw noticed the splint on Screech's leg. The crow hadn't complained once about the injury since Lydia had put it on.

"Let me think about it," said Caw.

Lydia rolled her eyes. "All right, think about it. Then come at seven o'clock." She gave him a wave and hurried off toward her house, pausing to call back. "Oh, and you might want to take a bath."

"I don't have a—"

But she was already gone.

Caw climbed the park gates, breaking a spiderweb that glistened between two bars. The silk strands clung to his fingers. On his own again, he felt a little strange. He was used to being alone—he told himself—so if anything, he should feel relieved. But somehow, he couldn't get himself to be glad that Lydia was gone. He brushed away the webbing.

Thank goodness we shook her off, said Glum. *Let's get back to the nest and have a nice nap, shall we?*

As Caw reached the bottom of his tree, his eyes caught a movement, something scurrying away into a bush.

Was that a rat? said Screech.

"I think it was a mouse," said Caw.

Same difference, said Glum. *They're all dinner.*

Caw pulled his T-shirt collar up to his nose and sniffed. "What did she mean, 'take a bath'?"

You're not going to go, are you? said Glum, already settling on a low branch.

"No," said Caw, as he started to climb. "Well, maybe."

6

Glum perched up ahead on the side-view mirror of Mr. Strickham's car. *It's not too late to turn back,* he said.

Caw steeled himself and kept walking. In the distance, the bells of Blackstone Cathedral were ringing out seven o'clock. The sun still peeked above the trees, throwing Caw's long shadow ahead of him, but already the foxes had started prowling. Caw saw one darting through the bushes as he approached the Strickhams' house.

We could go and raid the Dumpsters, said Screech. *Rich pickings!*

"I want to do this," he told them.

You don't look like it, said Glum. *You're all pale.*

Caw tried to ignore them. It didn't matter whether he wanted to come or not—he felt like he owed it to Lydia. She might be a bit pushy, but she'd come to the library with him, *and* she'd mended Screech's leg.

As he reached the doorstep, he saw his reflection distorted in the huge polished knocker. He gave his armpit a quick sniff. He'd washed as well as he could in pond water and flattened his hair with an old comb, but he still felt like a fraud. At least he'd managed to find a new pair of shoes. Someone had thrown them out in a garbage can. They were a size too small, and one had a hole in the toe, so Caw had cut the end off the other one to make them match. From his suitcase he'd selected a black T-shirt, only slightly torn at the collar. It had a paint stain on the back, but as long as he didn't take off his long black coat, no one would know.

He lifted the knocker, heart beating fast. Then froze.

What was he thinking?

"I can't do this," he muttered. He let the knocker down gently and backed away.

He's seen sense! said Screech, tapping his talons on the top of Mr. Strickham's car. *So what's it going to be? Indian food? Chinese?*

The door opened suddenly, making Caw's heart leap, and there stood Lydia, wearing some sort of green woolen dress. She looked tidy and clean. Much cleaner than Caw. "I knew you'd come!" she said.

Before he could say anything, she grabbed his arm and tugged him into the house, leaving the squawking crows outside. Immediately Lydia's dog, Benjy, began sniffing around his ankles. Benjy was white with brown patches and had bulgy eyes and floppy ears. Caw found himself at the bottom of a wide staircase, standing on a thick, pale carpet. He saw in horror that his shoes had already left a black smudge of dirt on it. "I'm sorry!" he said. "I'll take them off."

As he slipped his feet out, a memory of the dream came back, and of the carpet at his parents' house—bare skin sinking into luxurious softness—until he noticed Lydia looking down at his shoes and fighting a smile. "Come on!" she said. "Dinner's almost ready."

She led him down a hallway lined with framed photographs, Benjy trotting alongside. The pictures were all of the Strickham family. There were beautiful porcelain-and-glass lamps giving off a soft green light. But it was the smell that Caw noticed the most. The aroma of food made his mouth water so much he was scared he might drool on the carpet.

At the far end, a set of double doors opened onto a huge table with candles in the middle and plates laid out. Caw could hardly believe, after watching so many times through the window, that he was finally inside. The warmth and softness seemed to draw him forward.

Sitting at one end of the table reading a newspaper, a pair of spectacles perched at the end of his nose, was Mr. Strickham.

"Dad?" said Lydia.

Mr. Strickham turned, then started. "What the . . ." His mouth opened and closed and he stood up, staring at Caw. "Lydia, what's this boy doing here?"

With a horrible sinking feeling, Caw's eyes swept over the table. It was set for three.

"I invited him," said Lydia. "To say thank you."

"You *invited* him?" said Mr. Strickham.

"I'll go," said Caw, turning.

Lydia grabbed him. "No, you won't," she said. "Will he, Dad?"

She glared at her father, whose eyes settled on Caw's bare feet before returning to his face.

"And your name is?" he said.

"He's called Caw," said Lydia. "Caw, this is my father."

Lydia's dad took another second before he nodded briskly and held out a hand. He seemed to be doing his best to smile. Caw took the hand, glad that he'd given his nails a thorough scrub in the pond.

At that moment, a woman entered the room, holding a steaming dish. She was slim, with softly curling red hair that she had pulled back into a loose bun, and she wore a pink apron over a pale dress. Caw recognized her at once. Lydia's mother. Her eyes flashed wide in alarm when she saw him. "Who are you?" she said.

"It seems Lydia has brought a . . . ah . . . this . . . friend for dinner," said Mr. Strickham.

"He's our *guest*," said Lydia. "He's Caw. The boy who was there last night."

"I see," said Mrs. Strickham, narrowing her gaze. Caw began to feel uncomfortable under her intense stare.

"We at least owe him dinner," said Lydia. "I'll get another plate."

She gestured to a chair. "Caw, sit there."

As Lydia left the room, Caw thought about turning and running away. They didn't want him here, obviously. He should have listened to Glum and Screech. He tried to offer a smile, but he was pretty sure it came out more like a grimace. Mr. Strickham nodded as though he wasn't sure how to respond. His wife just placed the dish gently on the table.

"Please, take a seat," said Lydia's father.

Caw did as he was told, leaving his hands at his sides as he sat down. Everything looked so clean! The walls, the floor, the tablecloth . . . He hardly dared move for fear of spreading dirt.

Lydia soon returned, and everyone took their places at the table. Mrs. Strickham lifted the lid off a platter to reveal a joint of meat. The smell made Caw's mouth fill up with saliva all over again. He swallowed nervously.

"So, where do you live, Caw?" asked Mr. Strickham as he carved the meat with a huge knife.

"Nearby."

"With your parents?" asked Mr. Strickham.

"No," said Caw. "I live alone."

Mr. Strickham's expression suddenly turned severe. "You don't look old enough," he said.

Lydia's eyes darted to her father. Caw's heart thumped with a rush of panic, and he racked his brains. If they found out he was only thirteen, they'd call the authorities.

"He's sixteen," said Lydia.

"Really?" said Mr. Strickham. "I only ask because—"

"I am," lied Caw. "I'm sixteen."

"Stop interrogating him, Dad," said Lydia. She laid a plate in front of Caw, heaped with meat, potatoes, and vegetables, all smothered in gravy. "Dig in," she said.

Caw looked up, and Mrs. Strickham nodded. She seemed a little pale, he noticed. "I hope you like it," she said.

Caw picked up a slice of meat and sank his teeth in. He almost groaned in pleasure. It was like nothing he'd ever tasted, soft in texture and almost sweet. He took another bite, and the sauce dribbled over his hands. He bit into a potato and almost had to spit it out because it was so hot. He opened his mouth and sucked in breaths of cold air before chewing furiously and swallowing. Then he took a handful of something green and pushed it in as well. The flavors mingled wonderfully. Some fell out onto his plate, so he crammed it back in. He swallowed thickly again and licked the rich sauce off his fingers and his wrist.

It was quiet at the table, he realized, and when he looked up he saw all three members of the Strickham family staring at him, openmouthed. They were holding knives and forks. Caw blushed to the roots of his hair.

"He's not used to company," said Lydia quickly.

"Sorry," said Caw. "This is delicious." He picked up the knife and fork, but they felt all wrong in his hands. Mrs. Strickham watched him curiously, slowly slicing her food and placing a small morsel in her mouth.

The dinner proceeded in silence. Caw barely looked up, and though he tried to pace himself, he soon finished what was on his plate. Lydia gave him more without asking.

"You seem hungry, Caw," said Mr. Strickham. "When was the last time you ate?"

Caw thought back to the apples and chocolate Lydia had given him. "Earlier today," he said.

"You know, I might be able to find you some . . . support," said Mr. Strickham, laying down his knife and fork.

Caw frowned.

"The city can look after children who haven't—"

"I'm *sixteen*," said Caw, a little too loudly.

"There's no need to be aggressive," said Mr. Strickham. "I'm only trying to help you."

"Leave him alone, Dad," said Lydia.

Mr. Strickham shot her a glare. "Don't raise your voice at me, young lady. Not after your disobedience last night."

"Without Caw and his crows, we'd be *dead*," said Lydia. "I just think we should respect his privacy."

Mr. Strickham seemed about to say something, then shook his

head. "You're right, Lydia." He smiled at Caw. "I'm sorry."

"Did you say *crows*, dear?" Mrs. Strickham asked.

"Yes," Lydia answered. "Caw has these three tame crows that hang around him. Two of them attacked the prisoner in the alley last night."

"How very strange," Mrs. Strickham said. Her brow furrowed, and she cleared her throat. "I'm going to the bathroom. If you'll excuse me." She stood up and dabbed the corner of her mouth with a crisp napkin, then left the room.

Caw noticed a movement at the window—a fluttering of wings. It was Screech, perched outside. His heart sank. That was the last thing he needed—just when he seemed to have won them over. Caw gave a jerk of his hand, to say, *Go away!*

A sudden barking sounded from the hallway.

"Quiet down, Benjy!" called Mr. Strickham. "So, Caw, have you always lived in Blackstone?"

The barks became frantic.

"What's gotten into him?" said Lydia. She stood up and walked out of the room. Not alone *again*, thought Caw.

But a second later Lydia gave a piercing scream.

"Lydia!" shouted Mr. Strickham. He was on his feet at the same time as Caw, both rushing toward the hall.

Caw skidded to a halt, trying to work out what he was seeing. Benjy cowered at the bottom of the stairs, barking madly, as Lydia screamed and screamed.

Lying on the carpet was a snake. Gray-scaled and about ten feet long, its body was coiled, but its stubby head lifted from the ground. Mr. Strickham grabbed Caw as he tried to spring forward. "No, stay back!" he said.

"Get away from my dog!" Lydia cried. "Benjy!"

The snake darted forward, and Benjy's bark became a whimper as its fangs caught his leg and held on. The dog growled and snapped and rolled until he squirmed free. With a hiss, the snake turned and slithered straight at Lydia, its gleaming jade eyes watching her every movement.

Caw tore his arm from Mr. Strickham's grip. He seized the lamp standing in the hallway, tugged its cord free of the socket, and threw it at the snake. Glass and china exploded across the floor. Caw seized another lamp and hefted it above his head. The scaly creature darted away, toward an open vent in the wall. Before anyone could stop it, it slid into the darkness.

Caw put the lamp down. His blood was pumping hard.

"Benjy?" murmured Lydia. She crouched beside her dog. He was lying on his side, eyes staring, panting rapidly. Two tooth marks were horribly visible in his leg, oozing blood.

Mr. Strickham slammed the vent cover back against the wall. He tightened the screws, just as his wife came rushing into the hall. "What's going on?" she asked in a high-pitched voice. Her eyes took in the remains of the lamp, then Benjy and Lydia, and finally Caw.

"It was a snake," said Mr. Strickham. "I've never seen anything like it. Where did it come from?"

Mrs. Strickham glared at Caw, as though it was somehow his fault, then walked to Lydia's side. "Was he bitten?" she said.

Lydia nodded, tears streaming down her face as she cradled her dog. "He's hardly breathing!"

Caw watched as the dog's body trembled and twitched, then suddenly sagged over Lydia's knees. The dog's big eyes kept staring, but the light was gone from them.

"Benjy!" whispered Lydia.

Mrs. Strickham put a hand on her daughter's back. "I'm so sorry, sweetheart," she said.

"No!" said Lydia. "Call the vet!"

Mrs. Strickham pulled her daughter into an embrace as the dog lay limp across her lap. "He's gone," she said, hugging her daughter as she wept. "He's gone."

Caw just stood there, feeling helpless.

Mr. Strickham had one hand pressed against his forehead, as if he couldn't quite believe what had happened. At last he gestured toward the door, looking at Caw. "I'm sorry, but we need to be alone."

Caw nodded, stunned into silence. He'd seen a grass snake or two in the park before—Glum said they were a delicacy—but never anything that size, and never anything poisonous. Not in Blackstone. He wanted to comfort Lydia too, but Mr. Strickham was already ushering him out.

"Thank you for dinner," stammered Caw, gathering up his shoes. "If there's anything I can—"

The door closed behind him.

Screech and Glum were waiting by the car. *We tried to warn you,* said Screech. *We saw the snake go in through the drain.*

We got it, though, said Glum. *Look!* He twitched his beak, gesturing to the ground beside the car. The snake lay in an S shape, lifeless, blood spreading out from its body.

Too late for Benjy.

Caw turned from the dead snake and stumbled down the path, leaving the crows behind, his mind still working.

Hey, where are you going? called Glum indignantly.

The snake had come up through the drain. Someone must have let it loose in there. Suddenly he heard footsteps, receding fast. Caw swerved into the road, heart thumping. It took his eyes a moment to adjust to the darkness, but as they did he saw a shape in the distance, running down the sidewalk away from Lydia's house. A tall, dark figure. His heart froze.

A young woman with black hair.

The escaped prisoner.

7

As the morning sun filtered through the trees, Caw was aching but wide awake. His skin tingled in the chill air.

He'd spent the night in the branches opposite the Strickhams' house, despite Glum and Screech urging him to return to the nest. He hadn't slept a wink. What if the woman returned? Or Jawbone or the creepy little man? Caw remembered Jawbone's fearlessness in the alley. The venomous snake was gone now, its body dropped in a hidden flower bed in the park by Glum and Screech. But it couldn't be a coincidence—the prisoners must have set it loose. Obviously they wanted revenge on Warden Strickham.

The sun rose higher in the sky, and still there was no sign of movement from the house.

Well, I am glad we sat here all night, said Glum with a disgruntled warble. *Not to mention all morning too. Can we go get some sleep now?*

Screech was huddled farther along the branch. *Please, Caw. Let's go back to the nest.*

"Soon," said Caw, stretching his arms.

You can't stay here all day! said Screech.

Caw didn't want to leave. But it didn't look as though the Strickhams were going to show themselves. Besides, the crow was right—the prisoners probably wouldn't attack in broad daylight.

"All right," he muttered at last. "Come on."

Just as he reached the top of the park wall, Lydia's bedroom curtains swept open. She stood there in her pajamas, looking right at him. From her gray face, he guessed that she hadn't slept much either. Her eyes were red-rimmed, as though she'd been crying.

She mouthed, "Wait there!" and closed the curtains again.

"Change of plan," Caw told the crows.

A few minutes later, Lydia came out of the house, dressed in her jeans, sneakers, a green top, and a puffy white sleeveless coat. Caw slipped down from the wall. "I'm sorry about Benjy," he said.

For a moment Lydia's face crumpled, but she blinked the tears back. "It's not your fault," she said softly. "I just don't understand. Where did that snake come from?"

"I saw someone last night," said Caw. He didn't want to scare Lydia, but he couldn't keep it from her either. "Right after I left. I think it was one of the prisoners—a woman, running away from your house."

"Here?" said Lydia. "Why didn't you tell us?"

"I— I didn't want to intrude," said Caw. "Your dad had just told me to leave."

69

Lydia's lips pressed together. "You think she had something to do with the snake?" she said.

"Maybe," said Caw. "I've never seen a snake like that in Blackstone before."

"I have, but only in the zoo," said Lydia. "Mom thought it might have escaped." She looked back up at the house. "I'm scared. Dad's had threats before, but nothing like this."

Caw wanted to comfort her, but he didn't know how. So instead he changed the subject. "We should go to the library," he said. "Maybe Miss Wallace found out something about that spider."

"Good thinking," said Lydia. "It might even help Dad track down the prisoners."

Hold up, said Screech, from the wall above. *You're not seriously going to hang around with her, are you? She's dangerous! Her and her dad.*

Lydia looked up at the crow's sound.

"Oh, I didn't see them there," she said. "Hello, crows!"

Screech is right, said Glum, peering down at Lydia with disapproval. *I vote we go back to the nest and lie low until this has all blown over.*

Caw felt a surge of anger but kept his voice steady. "I'm going," he said. "That's the end of it."

Lydia cast a glance at the crows. "They don't like me, do they?" she said.

"It's not that," said Caw. "They're just worried about me."

I'm serious, said Glum. *Nothing good can come of this spider business. Why can't you forget it?*

Caw rounded on the bird. "Look, Glum, do you know something you're not telling me? Because if you do, spit it out."

Glum turned his head away. *All I know is that Milky spoke yesterday,* said the crow. *And that never happens. He may have lost his marbles, but I didn't like what he said.*

Lydia was looking confused. "Glum?" she said. "Is that his name?"

Caw took a deep breath. "I think that prisoner had something to do with my parents," he said calmly to the crows. "You can't expect me to sit in a tree my whole life and just forget about them." For once, the crows were silent.

Glum twitched his beak. *Do what you think you have to,* he said.

Caw had grown used to Glum's moods over the years. The old crow could be stubborn, but this was different. He seemed almost hurt.

Well, too bad. Caw didn't need looking after.

"Come on," he said to Lydia. "Let's go."

They'd walked halfway along the side of the park when Caw realized the crows hadn't followed. He looked back and saw Glum and Screech both perched where he'd left them, watching.

Then it hit him. *They're jealous of Lydia. They're annoyed that I'm not relying on them for once.*

"Is everything okay?" asked Lydia.

"It's fine," said Caw, his voice cold. He turned away from his crows and kept walking. It was time he stood up to them and did things on his own terms.

From the park there were several routes into the city. Caw tended to clamber across the rooftops, following the back alleys or the rail tracks, but today they took the main street lined with warehouses and auto-repair shops. For a while, he was silent, stewing over his argument with the crows, wondering if he should have said anything differently. But as they reached the edges of the city, where the tall apartment buildings and shops began to appear, Lydia broke the silence.

"You know, when you said you spoke to crows, I didn't really get it," she said. "But you actually *speak* with them, don't you? You really understand what they're saying."

"Yes," said Caw. "Ever since they . . ." Ever since a murder of crows took him away from his parents, he'd been about to say, but he didn't know how she'd react to that.

"You can tell me," Lydia said. She placed a hand on his arm, and he managed not to flinch away.

"I've never told anyone."

"Try me," she replied. "Please. I need something to take my mind off Benjy."

Caw glanced at her to check that she wasn't smiling. She looked back, her face open and honest. He stopped walking and took a deep breath. Was he really ready to share this now? "They've always looked after me," he said slowly. "I can't remember much before the crows."

"But you remember something?" she said.

Caw bit his lip. He'd already trusted Lydia with more secrets than he'd ever confided in anyone else—why not this?

"The dream I have," he began. "Like I told you, it feels more like a memory." He thought he'd feel foolish saying it out loud, but as he told her about the crows carrying him away from the open window, about his parents abandoning him, she listened carefully.

Before Caw knew it, he was telling her more, about the early days, when the nest was barely big enough to hold him, about how the different crows had come and gone, about gradually exploring more and more of Blackstone.

As the words spilled out of him, about how hard it had been, how lonely, he felt the old familiar feeling building in his chest. Anger at his parents for *making* it so hard. Why couldn't they have kept him close and loved him like real parents? He saw how Mrs. Strickham had hugged Lydia when Benjy was dying, heard the despair in her father's voice during the alley fight when he thought she was in danger. How could his parents have done what they did? All the times he'd gone hungry, or taken a fall from the branches, when he'd shivered with cold on wintry nights . . . Where were they?

"Hey, Caw, are you okay?" said Lydia.

Caw realized his fingers were balled into fists. It took a few seconds to let the anger drain away. "Yes," he said. "I'm sorry."

He felt her hand creep into his and give it a squeeze. "I understand," she said. "You're welcome at our house, anytime."

Caw smiled. "I'm not sure your parents would say that."

But Lydia's eyes had focused on something past him. It was a newspaper kiosk. "Check it out!" she said. She walked over, picked up a paper, paid the man inside, then came hurrying back. She unfolded it so Caw could see.

The words meant nothing to Caw, other than the one at the top of the page—*BLACKSTONE*, which matched the park gates. The pictures were clear enough, though—the faces of the three escaped convicts. Lydia pointed at the one with the tattoo. "His name is Clarence Trap, aka Jawbone," she said. "The woman is Eleanor Kreuss, and the small one is called Ernest Vetch." Her eyes scanned the tiny writing. "It says all three were jailed in the Dark Summer for crimes including murder, robbery, and kidnapping. They were serving life sentences with no chance of parole. I guess that's why they were in maximum security."

"What's the Dark Summer?" asked Caw.

Lydia looked at him like he'd just asked which way the sky was.

"You really have been keeping to yourself, haven't you?" she said. "The Dark Summer was this crime wave that happened back when we were about five or six. Tons of attacks and unexplained murders, all over Blackstone. Packs of wild animals roaming the streets. Really weird stuff. Apparently Blackstone was pretty nice before then—at least that's what my dad says. He says the city never recovered."

Caw let the information sink in. His heart began to race. "How many years ago?"

Lydia's brow wrinkled. "Maybe . . . seven or eight?"

"Eight years," said Caw. "That was when my parents sent me away." The Dark Summer, his parents, the escaped convicts. The spider.

"Really?" said Lydia. "Do you think it's a coincidence?"

Caw didn't answer. He quickened his stride, and Lydia jogged to keep up. He felt as though the threads of a mystery were starting to come together, connecting in a web that entangled every part of his life.

And at the center of that web lay a spider.

The benches outside the library were empty.

"That's weird," said Lydia. "There are normally loads of people here on a Saturday."

When they got to the top of the steps, Caw saw a sign hanging around the doors. Lydia stopped. "Oh, it's closed!"

"It can't be," said Caw. "Miss Wallace told us to come back today."

"Well, that's what the sign says. What do we do now?" asked Lydia.

"Let's check in back," said Caw. "That's where she normally leaves my books."

As they rounded the side of the library, a squirming, sick sensation began to build in the bottom of Caw's stomach.

Miss Wallace's car was parked in its usual space. He knew the little blue vehicle was hers because he'd watched her drive in on days that he arrived early, anxious for his weekly cup of hot chocolate.

Dread welled up through his chest. And as they reached the fire-exit steps, he saw that there was something spray-painted across the wall.

Lydia gasped, and her hand shot to her mouth.

Caw suddenly felt very cold. "No," he mumbled. "Please . . . not Miss Wallace."

It was a spider, freshly drawn, the paint still glistening. Just like the one in his dream.

Caw jumped down to the bottom of the steps by the side door and tried the handle. It wasn't locked. He put his finger to his lips and stepped inside.

Utter silence reigned within. The light was on in Miss Wallace's office, and the door was ajar. Caw peered in. No one.

"Maybe we should call the police," whispered Lydia.

"Not yet," said Caw.

The main lights in the library were off, but there was a strange smell in the air. It reminded Caw of the park after heavy rain. Damp and earthy like dead leaves.

He rounded the shelves at the back of the library. There! Miss Wallace. Relief flooded through him. She was sitting at her desk, side-on to him, her glasses hanging around her neck.

"Miss Wallace!" he called, walking over.

She didn't move.

"Miss Wallace?" Caw said more quietly.

As he reached the front of the desk, horror gripped him by the throat. Behind him, Lydia gave a small moan. Miss Wallace was sitting upright, looking straight at them with eyes wide open and unfocused. Something was wrong with her mouth. Pale silvery threads covered her lips and nose like a mask. Spider silk. Trails of blood had dripped down from her face onto her cream blouse, creating a macabre design in shades of crimson.

Caw felt dizzy, and the room seemed to wobble. It was like something from a nightmare leeching into the real world.

Lydia's voice brought everything back into focus. "Is she . . . dead?" she said.

Caw went to Miss Wallace's side. Her odd, lifeless expression made her resemble a shop mannequin. He could hardly bear to look into her eyes, once so full of kindness. He checked her wrist to make sure. No pulse. Her skin felt cold and waxy.

"Why?" he said. "Miss Wallace never hurt anybody. She helped people."

Caw sank to her side. As he did so, he noticed that one of her hands was clenched tightly, and inside he caught a glimpse of something white.

"There's something here," he said. "She must have been holding it when she was . . ." It was too horrible to say.

Lydia came around the desk, hovering as though she was afraid to approach the body. Caw gently loosened Miss Wallace's fingers, and a ball of paper fell free. As he opened it, he realized what it was—Lydia's drawing of the spider. His pulse began to race, and his mouth went dry. There was a single word written beneath the image. He looked up at Lydia.

"'Quaker,'" she read. "What does that mean?"

"I don't know," whispered Caw. His eyes were drawn back to the mask of white strands across Miss Wallace's face. He felt sick imagining how she must have struggled for breath.

"I'm phoning the police," said Lydia. She went to the desk and picked up the receiver, then frowned. "There's no dial tone."

A booming laugh echoed through the still air. Caw whirled around and saw the big prisoner—Jawbone—standing on the balcony above. He'd swapped his prison garb for a bloodred T-shirt and black jeans. Light from the windows caught his gleaming bald head, so Caw could make out the thick plates of his skull beneath the skin. His tattoo stretched from ear to ear, looking even more clown-like and chilling than before.

"You!" said Caw.

"Joining the party, boy?" barked the prisoner.

Suddenly Lydia grabbed Caw's arm and pointed. "Look!"

The dark-haired woman was approaching from the back of the library. She wore a black gown that covered her from head to toe, her hair pulled into a thick ponytail that curled once around her neck like a black scarf, then hung over her shoulder. In her hand she held a long, silver sewing needle. "Don't worry, children," she said. "I was gentle with her."

Caw's anger almost broke through his fear. He and Lydia ran toward Miss Wallace's office, but a stunted shape scurried across their path. He was wearing a beige trench coat, at least two sizes too big.

"Scuttle, at your service," said the man, licking his lips grotesquely. "I believe you've met my associates Jawbone and Mamba."

Caw shot a look toward the front doors, and his heart sank as he saw a huge chain looped through the handles, fastened with a padlock.

They were trapped.

8

"Nowhere to run, children," said Mamba.

"Why did you kill her?" shouted Caw, pointing to Miss Wallace's limp body. "She never hurt anyone!"

"We had to," said Jawbone. His grin widened. "Not that we didn't enjoy it." He looked at the others. "Let's finish the job, shall we?"

The short man sniggered and snapped his fingers.

Caw heard a strange chattering sound, and then something dropped from the cuff of Scuttle's trench coat. It darted across the ground. A cockroach.

Lydia stumbled back into Caw. "Gross!"

"There are more where that came from," said Scuttle.

He closed his eyes, as if he was praying. Then insects began to pour from both sleeves of his coat in a hideous wave of black shells and wriggling legs. Hundreds of cockroaches, climbing down his clothes and landing on the floor. Caw gasped as they fell from Scuttle's trouser legs too, piling on top of one another in an endless stream.

"Caw?" said Lydia, her voice a terrified whisper.

"That's not possible," he murmured. Where were they coming from?

The roaches swarmed across the floor, straight toward them, and Lydia screamed. Caw grabbed her hand and yanked her toward a side door. The cockroaches veered after them in a squealing, rustling mass.

They'd almost reached the door when Lydia yelped, "Caw, stop!"

Caw skidded to a halt as she tugged him back. Then he made out movement in the corridor beyond the door. Three huge shapes emerged, padding through the doorway. They were dogs, their bodies thick with muscle beneath short fur, with yellow eyes glaring over wrinkled snouts. Deep growls reverberated from their chests, and drool spilled from black lips drawn up over jagged teeth.

As the cockroaches swept toward them, Caw jumped onto a table and pulled Lydia up beside him. She gripped his arm hard, her eyes full of panic.

"Cockroaches can climb, you know!" she said.

The black slick of insects covered the table legs and crept over the edge. Caw kicked at them, scattering the first wave onto the floor. But more followed, closing from all sides. Lydia jumped, landing with a crunch among them, and Caw leaped after her. His feet sank into the broken shells. Almost straightaway, the roaches climbed over his feet and legs, in a tickling, scratching tide.

Caw hopped to the edge of the seething mass, crushing more

with every step. He heard Lydia scream again, and then something slammed into his side and he fell. Foul breath washed over him as he realized it was one of the dogs. Its forepaws pinned his arms, and its weight crushed the air out of him. The dog's jaws snapped and snarled inches from his face. He was sure at any second it would sink those teeth into the soft flesh of his cheek. He felt the cockroaches scurry off him, as if even they were afraid.

"I wouldn't move, if I were you," said Jawbone. Caw turned his head away from the teeth and saw that Lydia was pinned down too. The third dog was sitting obediently at Jawbone's side, licking his hand. "My dogs could tear through your throat like cotton candy."

The dog on top of Caw lowered its snout and growled. Caw froze, his eyes glued shut. He could sense the dog's vicious hunger. It wanted nothing more than to rip him to shreds, but something was holding it in check.

The woman's voice came next. "No crows to help you this time," she said.

Caw opened his eyes again and saw her standing beside Lydia, eyeing her like a curious specimen. Lydia's chest was rising and falling rapidly, and her features twisted in disgust. A snake, just like the one that had killed Benjy, was coiled around Mamba's arm. Its neck and head rested on her wrist, and she stroked its scales with the points of her long black nails. Its tongue flickered, shivering in delight.

"What have you done to them?" cried Scuttle.

He was crouched over a patch of squashed cockroaches, scooping them into his hands and letting their broken bodies fall through his fingers. Tears ran down his face. The rest of the roaches seemed to have vanished as quickly as they'd arrived.

Who *were* these people?

The hunchbacked man glared at Caw and Lydia, eyes wet and angry. "Let me kill them!" he snapped. "Let my little ones crawl into their mouths and eat them from the inside!"

He staggered toward them, but the third dog blocked his path, snarling, ears drawn back.

"Not now," said Jawbone. "Remember why we're here."

Not to kill us, then. Despite his fear, Caw tried to think clearly. *We'd be dead if that was their plan.*

The dog on top of Caw suddenly lifted its head, its ears cocked. The other dogs copied the motion.

A second later Caw heard sirens. Hope flickered in his heart.

"Cops!" hissed Mamba. "How did they know?"

Jawbone turned his massive head toward Miss Wallace's corpse. He grunted. "She must have pressed the panic button right before she died."

Cars screeched to a halt outside, and through the frosted glass of the windows Caw saw the flash of blue and red lights.

"Help!" yelled Lydia. "Help us!"

"What do we do?" Scuttle asked, eyes darting around.

The door of the library thudded and the chains rattled.

"We go," said Jawbone calmly. His eyes fell on Lydia. "Bring the girl."

Mamba and Scuttle rushed forward, and Caw felt the weight of the dog lift off his chest. He rolled over, just in time to see Scuttle haul Lydia off the ground and throw her over his shoulder. She kicked and screamed, her red hair falling over her face. Caw lunged after her, but a stinging blow caught him across the cheek and he fell back against Miss Wallace's desk, stunned. Mamba stood in front of him—he hadn't even seen her move, let alone strike him. Close up, he saw her face in more detail. Tall cheekbones, lips that were almost black. Eyes that glittered like precious jewels. She turned quickly and followed the others.

Jawbone reached into his pocket and pulled out something the size of an apple. He clicked a button on the top and tossed it spinning into the middle of the room. A rush of smoke poured out, spreading quickly from the ground up.

"Get off me!" cried Lydia.

Caw scanned Miss Wallace's desk and saw her paperweight. He snatched it up, took aim, and hurled it across the library. It hit Scuttle's head with a sickening thud and the man fell to his knees, letting go of Lydia. She scrambled away as Mamba rushed to Scuttle's side. Moments later they were hidden by smoke.

"That little wretch!" snarled Scuttle. "Where'd she go?"

"Leave her!" came Jawbone's voice. "We can't afford to get caught."

Caw heard a bang, and through a gap in the drifting smoke he saw the front doors burst open. A cop went down on one knee as light flooded in. Flashlight beams lit up the smoke, and shouts filled the air.

"Police!"

"Don't move!"

Caw froze beside Miss Wallace's body. He spotted Lydia's shadow moving between the shelves thirty feet away.

A flashlight dazzled him.

"Hands where I can see them!" yelled a cop.

Caw ducked and plunged into the waves of smoke. A single gunshot cracked, and the shelf beside his head exploded into splinters. Two more bullets whizzed past and smacked into the wall.

"Wait!" said Lydia.

By the time he reached her side, Caw could barely see a thing. He sucked in a lungful of the acrid smoke and coughed, his lungs burning.

"Come on!" he said, tugging Lydia toward the door the dogs had emerged from.

More shots ripped through the air overhead.

"Hold your fire!" shouted a voice. "There might be hostages!"

The gunfire stopped as Caw dragged Lydia along the corridor. They passed several doors before they reached a set of stairs leading downward. He took them three at a time, and Lydia stumbled after him. At the bottom Caw pushed open a door with a picture of a man on it and found himself in a bathroom. There were windows at head height over the sinks.

"Caw, stop!" said Lydia. "The police are on our side."

"No, they're not!" said Caw. He climbed up beside a sink and opened the window lever but couldn't budge the pane. He slammed a palm into it.

"We'll just explain what happened! They'll believe us!" said Lydia. She wasn't climbing up beside him.

"Help me!" said Caw, punching the window frame again. It gave a fraction.

Lydia looked back toward the door. "Caw, they'll think we're guilty of something if we run!"

Caw drew his hand back and whacked the window again. It opened about a foot, and dried paint flaked off the frame. He held out his hand to her. "Please, Lydia," he said. "You don't understand. If they take me in, I'll never get out again. They'll put me in an orphanage."

Lydia stared at him and softened. She knew it was true.

Caw took her hand and helped her up. "You first," he said.

Confused voices sounded from outside. "Take it one room at a time!"

"Extreme caution, they might be armed!"

"Room clear!"

Lydia squeezed through the gap, and Caw boosted himself after her. He heard the bathroom door slam open and dragged his body onto the gravel outside. He didn't look back as they ran across the parking lot, past Miss Wallace's car.

"Hey you!" cried a voice. "Stop!"

An engine revved and a police car slewed across their path. Two cops jumped out. One reached for his gun, but before it was out of the holster, Screech swooped down onto his arm. The cop jerked back with a wail of surprise as Glum snatched the hat from his head. Lydia ran past, toward an alleyway. The other cop spread his arms wide to catch Caw, bending slightly.

"You're not going anywhere, kid!" he said. Caw ran full pelt at him, and for a strange second he felt almost weightless, like he was a crow himself. He jumped high, his legs connecting with the policeman's shoulder, and the world turned upside down as he tumbled head over heels.

He landed on his back on the car hood, sliding off the far side. The cop turned, eyes wide in amazement, as Caw ran after Lydia with his coat billowing.

Moments later he heard the pounding feet of the cops close behind them.

An enormous flock of pigeons was feeding on the ground

ahead, and Caw plunged straight through them. The birds took flight in screeching panic, and when Caw looked back, he saw the cops fighting their way through the flapping wings.

Above them soared two black shapes—Glum and Screech.

"Which way?" said Lydia.

Screech and Glum veered left ahead. "Follow the crows!" said Caw, pointing.

They took the twisting alleys through the run-down riverside districts of Blackstone, with the crows always just ahead.

By the time they stopped running, they were by a junction with one of the main roads running north. Sirens occasionally wailed nearby, but they had lost the cops. Caw and Lydia were both panting hard. "That was . . . some jump," she said. "Sure you didn't spend time in the circus?"

Caw shook his head. He didn't know how he'd done it. He just . . . had.

Glum flapped to the ground at their feet, while Screech landed on the awning of a café opposite.

"You came," said Caw.

I didn't want to, said Glum, with a haughty lift of his beak, *but Screech convinced me. Lucky for you.*

"Tell them thank you," said Lydia.

Tell her we don't need her thanks, said Glum. *Caw, can't you see she's dangerous?*

"What did he say?" asked Lydia.

"He said, 'Think nothing of it,'" Caw lied.

Enough, Caw, said Glum. *This road leads back to the park. Say your good-byes.*

"We should go to my father," said Lydia. "He'll know what to do."

Absolutely not, said Glum. *Don't listen to her.*

"I can't," Caw said. "He won't understand."

Lydia blew a strand of hair out of her face. "Then we'll make him," she said. "He's not the police. He's not against you. And he's my dad!"

You can't trust him, said Glum.

Lydia flashed an annoyed glare at the crow, almost as if she understood his squawks.

"My dad's not interested in you, Caw," she said. "He wants those convicts."

Caw knew Mr. Strickham wasn't a bad man, but he wasn't a friend either.

"Don't you see?" Lydia urged. "We need people on our side. We don't have to face this on our own."

You're not on your own, said Glum. *You've got us.*

Caw shook his head and stared at the crow. "You saved us, Glum," he said. "I know you did, but there's something big going on here. They killed Miss Wallace. And that spider from my dream had something to do with it. It was painted on the wall, and . . . they put a spider's web over her mouth." He felt a lump in his throat. "She must have been so afraid," he murmured.

Glum cocked his head and looked upward. Caw followed his gaze and saw Milky for the first time, standing on the rim of a satellite dish.

"When did he get there?" asked Caw.

He's been watching all along, said Glum.

Milky gave a soft warble that Caw hadn't heard before.

Screech flew over and landed on Caw's shoulder. *Did you see the way I got that cop?* he said. *Kapow!*

"I saw," said Caw. He smiled sheepishly. "I'm sorry for what I said earlier. I don't deserve your help."

As they emerged onto the main street, Caw saw a pigeon standing on top of a street lamp.

"The pigeons helped too," he said, looking up into the bird's unblinking eyes. "Didn't they?"

A fluke, said Screech. He gave a couple of harsh squawks, and the pigeon took off.

Caw lost himself in his thoughts while they hurried toward Lydia's house. As the adrenaline of the chase seeped away, his heart became heavy.

"You're not to blame, you know," said Lydia, as though she'd guessed what he was thinking. They were both keeping a lookout for any sign of the police as they hurried down a deserted side street. The crows flew ahead to the road junctions, squawking twice if the way was clear, once if not. Caw and Lydia frequently ducked behind parked cars, just in case.

"She'd be alive if it weren't for me," said Caw. "I felt like we were being followed the first time we went to the library. It must have been those prisoners. Maybe if I hadn't asked her to help . . ."

At the back of his mind lurked another question. Who, or what, was Quaker? And why was the word so important that Miss Wallace had kept it in her hand, even as she was killed?

Lydia took hold of his arm. When he looked up, he saw her gaze pleading with him. "Caw, those three prisoners killed Miss Wallace, not you. And when the police get them, my dad will lock them up and make sure they never get out again. All right?"

Caw was grateful for her words, even if he didn't really feel convinced. He felt a sudden fierce rage burning through his chest. Those murderers deserved worse than a prison cell. A lot worse.

After a few more turns, the walls of the park appeared at the end of the road, and then the Strickhams' house came into view.

"Are you sure about this?" asked Caw, feeling suddenly apprehensive. "I mean, your parents don't exactly like me, do they?"

"It's not that," said Lydia. "You're just a bit . . . different."

Charming, said Glum, swooping overhead. *We'll wait here.*

The three crows landed in the branches of the beech tree, Milky a branch higher than the others. His pale eyes seemed to follow Caw. The day had turned chilly, with gray clouds amassing in the sky.

Mrs. Strickham flung open the door before they were halfway up the drive.

"Where have you been, young lady?" she asked.

"Mom, we need to speak to Dad," said Lydia.

"Your father is on the phone," said Mrs. Strickham. "And what is that boy doing here again?" Her eyes snagged on something beyond Caw, and she paled. Caw turned and saw that she was looking at the crows. "Get inside," she said.

Lydia walked up the steps.

"Just you, Lydia," said her mother as Caw tried to follow.

Lydia stopped. "He's my friend. I'm not coming in without him."

Caw felt a rush of pride. No one had called him a friend in his entire life.

Mrs. Strickham opened her mouth but hesitated, as though she wasn't sure what to say. Her expression shifted, and all of a sudden she looked more sad than angry.

Mr. Strickham appeared behind her, his phone to his ear. "Thanks, John," he was saying. "Keep me in the loop." He looked haggard as he hung up, but his face came alive when he saw his daughter. "Lydia—thank goodness you're safe." His eyes flicked over to Caw nervously, and he turned to his wife. "Detective Stagg says there's been some sort of . . . incident at the library. Apparently the commissioner's taking a particular interest in it."

"I know," said Lydia. "We were there."

Mr. Strickham did a double take at his daughter. "You were *what*?" he snapped.

Caw stepped forward, trying to look bold. "We saw the killers, sir. It was those escaped prisoners."

"Tony!" pleaded Mrs. Strickham. "This boy . . ."

"Let him in," said Mr. Strickham. "It sounds like the pair of you have some explaining to do." He muttered something to his wife and then turned back to Caw. "Would you mind sitting in the lounge while I talk to Lydia alone?" he said.

Caw nodded, and Mr. Strickham led him into another huge room, this one with plush sofas and a fire burning in the hearth. There was a set of glass doors leading to a wrought-iron balcony overlooking the back garden, and beyond that, the hulking shape of the prison. Mr. Strickham gestured to a sofa and switched on the TV as Mrs. Strickham came in with a glass of water. She handed it to Caw without a word, then left again. Mr. Strickham fiddled with the remote and the sound got louder. A woman was talking about fuel prices.

"I'll just be a minute," said Mr. Strickham. He left the room, closing the door behind him.

Caw sipped the water, trying to clear his head. What had those convicts wanted in the library? Not to kill them, that was for sure. But what they'd done to Miss Wallace showed how merciless they could be. How were they connected to the spider?

And what about "Quaker"?

The woman on the screen touched her ear, and a piece of paper was handed to her by someone out of shot.

"This just in," she said. "Police are reporting a suspicious death at Blackstone Central Library. The victim has been identified as Miss Josephine Wallace, head librarian for the last decade. Police are keeping an open mind as to motive at this time, but anyone with information should contact . . ."

A tapping at the glass balcony doors made Caw look up. Screech and Glum were perched on the railing of the balcony outside.

Caw went quickly to the glass doors. They were locked, and the keyhole was empty. He put his mouth to the small hole.

"What is it?" he said.

Milky's worried about you, said Screech. *He doesn't trust them.*

"Who? The Strickhams?" said Caw. "Did he say that?"

Sort of, said Screech.

"Sort of?" Caw said, rolling his eyes. "Look, I know you don't like Lydia, but she's on my side. And I think her father is too."

Really? said Glum. *In that case, why has he locked you in?*

Caw's blood ran cold. "He . . . he hasn't."

Try the door then, said Glum.

Caw left the balcony doors, crept around the sofa, and placed his fingers on the door handle. When he pressed, it didn't move.

9

Caw pushed harder to be sure. A chill crept across his skin.

He glanced back at the crows, and Glum cocked his head, as if to say, *Told you so.*

Caw pressed his ear against the door. With the noise of the TV it was hard to hear.

"... for the best ... ," Mr. Strickham was saying.

Lydia's voice was louder. "But it didn't have anything to do with Caw, I swear!"

Mrs. Strickham cut in. "You don't understand. When all this is cleared up, you'll thank us."

"Please, Dad, don't!"

"It's settled," said Mr. Strickham. "I'm calling Detective Stagg. We'll get a squad car out here."

"No!" said Lydia. "How could you?"

Caw's eyes traveled back to the locked balcony doors, and then he jumped over the sofa to the mantelpiece. It was lined with ornaments. There were three little pots—he turned them over swiftly. Where were the keys? He went to a tall dresser holding china and glassware. He opened a drawer halfway down, his hands rooting about, but there were only papers inside.

"No, no, no . . . ," he mumbled under his breath.

Then his eyes settled on a potted plant. He rushed over and picked it up. Nothing underneath. But the blue ceramic pot was heavy. Easily heavy enough.

He walked to the balcony doors, raising the pot to shoulder height. The crows must have known what he was planning, because they flapped skyward.

Caw hesitated. Could he really do this? Something was peering at him from the wall—a photo of Mr. Strickham shaking hands with a female police officer, looking pleased with himself.

Yes, he could.

The smash as the pot hit the glass seemed impossibly loud, and the whole pane fell out in jagged shards.

"What was that?" yelled Mrs. Strickham.

Heart thumping, Caw climbed through the remains of the glass doors, placed both hands on the balcony, and vaulted over. He landed in the grass below, then darted toward the far fence. As he scrambled to the top, he saw the side road leading to the park. To safety. He looked back, just as Mr. Strickham reached the balcony, his face livid. "You come back here!" he shouted.

Caw turned away, dropped to the other side and, out of sight, ran toward the park wall.

Two minutes later he heaved himself through the nest's trapdoor, panting heavily. Milky perched on the branch outside. Glum and Screech were waiting on the platform, huddled side by side and watching him cautiously, as if they could sense his mood.

Caw crawled to the edge of the nest and buried his head in his hands. Why had he agreed to go to Lydia's house again? He should have known not to let his guard down. And now he'd lost everything. Any chance of keeping his new friend was smashed, along with that window.

Don't worry, said Glum. *You've got us to look after you.*

Just like old times, Screech added.

Caw looked up at them, shaking his head. They didn't understand. They couldn't.

He had *no one.* Lydia's parents would probably keep her inside for weeks, and they would never let her come into the park again. The police would be all over the city looking for him, so it would be almost impossible to find food safely.

"I can't believe they betrayed me," said Caw. "Why didn't they listen to Lydia?"

She's just a child, said Glum. *You're better off staying well away from that family.*

Caw felt hollow. "Maybe you're right," he said.

"Hello, crow talker," said a man's voice.

Caw almost leaped into the air, pressing himself against the side of the nest. The crows went wild, screeching and flapping as the curtain across the center of the nest was pulled aside. "What the . . . ?" Caw cried.

A dirt-smeared face peered at him. It was the homeless man— the one who'd rescued him from the gang outside the restaurant. He was here, crouched in the nest. His blue eyes glinted with curiosity.

"Get out!" shouted Caw, raising his fists. Screech and Glum flew in front of him, snapping with their beaks.

"Don't be alarmed," said the man, batting the air with his fingerless gloves. "I'm not here to hurt you."

"How did you get in here?" said Caw. He glared at Screech and Glum. "Why didn't you warn me?"

He must have sneaked in when we were at the house, said Glum, letting out a flurry of hostile squawks.

Caw frowned, puzzled. "But Milky was—"

"The white crow knows I'm here," said the man.

"He *what*?" said Caw.

"My associate, Pip, he's been keeping an eye on you. Please, crow talker, we have much to discuss."

"Stop calling me that! My name is Caw."

"Is it?" said the man, smiling strangely. "But you talk to crows, don't you?"

Caw was breathing heavily. "Yes," he said. "So what?"

"'So what' indeed! You say it like it's nothing special. You know others who can speak with animals, do you?"

Caw's heart was beginning to slow. "No," he admitted. But for a moment, he thought of the prisoners in the library. Those dogs, the cockroaches, and the snake . . .

The man snapped his fingers, and two pigeons hopped out from behind him.

Get out of our nest! said Screech.

"Meet my friends," said the man. "On my left is Blue. On my right, Sleektail. You were lucky she spotted you before you ran into those kids behind the restaurant. More lucky than you know." The pigeons both warbled. "And my name is Crumb."

"You can talk to them?" said Caw.

Of course he can't, said Screech. *Pigeons only understand one thing. Peck, peck, peck. All day long.*

"Since the day my father died, I've heard their voices," said Crumb. "Twelve years or thereabouts. This is a nice place, by the way." He pushed the tarpaulin with his fingertips. "Could do with more headroom, but it's cozy."

Milky flapped under the gap at the end of the tarpaulin, squawking.

Someone's coming! said Glum.

Crumb leaped into a crouch, faster than Caw would have thought possible. Silently, he prized back one edge of the tarp and peered over the side.

Caw scrambled to the hatch and looked down. Through the mesh of branches he saw Lydia at the base of the trunk.

"Caw?" she called.

Crumb put a dirty finger to his lips.

"Caw, are you up there?" said Lydia. "I just want to talk."

"Who is she?" whispered Crumb.

One of the pigeons cooed, and Crumb looked sideways at it.

"From the library?" he said.

The pigeon bobbed its head and cooed again. Crumb frowned.

"Please, Caw," said Lydia. "I just want to say I'm sorry. It was a misunderstanding."

Caw's anger flared, and he flung open the hatch. "Your dad was going to hand me over to the police!"

Lydia's head dropped. "I know. He made a big mistake. He just thought it was for the best."

"The best for who?" shouted Caw. He couldn't believe she was trying to make excuses. "Not for me, that's for sure."

"Can I come up?" asked Lydia.

No way, José, said Screech.

Not a chance! said Glum.

"I don't think that would be a good idea," said Caw. "Your parents don't trust me." He looked at the others. Glum was nodding in a satisfied way. "We can't be friends, Lydia," Caw added. Every word felt wrong.

Lydia was quiet for a long moment. "Please, Caw, you don't understand," she said at last. "My dad—he hasn't called the police. He promised he wouldn't. Can I come up?"

Don't trust her, said Glum.

Caw glanced at Crumb.

"I wouldn't," he said, "but it's your nest."

Caw tried to think straight. Sure, Lydia's parents might not like him, but Lydia herself—well, she'd only tried to be his friend.

He might regret it later, but he couldn't just cut her off.

"Come up," he said. "You know the way."

"Thanks!" she said, and Caw could hear the relief in her voice. Crumb shrank back to the other side of the nest with his pigeons, as the branches began to shake gently. Finally Lydia appeared in the hatch, pulling herself inside.

When she caught sight of Crumb, she yelped and clambered over to Caw.

"Who's that?" she said.

"Lydia, meet Crumb," said Caw.

Crumb unfolded his long limbs and held out a hand, the nails caked with dirt. He inclined his head in a small bow. "Pleased to meet you, Lydia."

Lydia looked at the hand for a fraction of a second before taking it. "Are you a friend of Caw's?"

"More of an acquaintance," he said. "Are *you* a friend of Caw's?"

Lydia looked hard at Caw. "I hope so," she said. "Caw, I know you don't trust the police, but maybe we should consider talking to them."

"I told you, I can't," said Caw. "They'll take me away. From the crows. From the nest. This is my life."

You tell her! said Screech with an emphatic nod of his beak.

"But they won't stop looking for you," said Lydia. "You'll be in tomorrow's papers, on the evening news." Her eyes were pleading. "You'll be hunted down."

"Then I'll leave," said Caw desperately. "Find another nest, in another city." Glum and Screech looked at him with surprise.

"And how will you get there?" said Lydia. "You can't drive, you can't take public transportion. You wouldn't make it a mile without someone calling the police."

Caw slumped. He knew she was right. And besides, he missed his park after being gone only a few hours—leaving Blackstone was a ridiculous idea.

Suddenly a pigeon burst into the nest, shrieking.

"What?" said Crumb, his pale eyes alert. "Where?"

A terrible realization hit Caw in the gut. Why was Lydia even here? Her parents would have been watching her like a hawk. "How come your dad let you leave the house, Lydia?" he said fiercely.

"Caw, come down!" called a voice from below.

Lydia's eyes went wide with shock. "Dad?" she said.

Caw felt like his heart was breaking. "You *led* him here?"

"No!" said Lydia, her face pale. "No, I didn't!"

Caw stared at her, but she shook her head. "I promise, Caw. He must have followed me."

Caw peered out of his nest, and his heart sank like a stone. There were policemen there—at least three of them surrounding the tree, as well as Mr. Strickham.

"I see the boy!" said one of the officers, a hand on his gun.

"Leave that alone!" said Mr. Strickham sharply. "He's just a kid. And my daughter's up there, for God's sake."

The officer left the gun in its holster.

"Caw," called Mr. Strickham. "These men are friends of mine. They won't hurt you, I promise. We can work this out together, but you have to come down."

Crumb laid a hand on Caw's shoulder. "Those people can't help you. The enemies we're facing—they're our own kind. They're *ferals*."

The word hung in the air, carrying with it something ancient, something powerful. It was strangely familiar, even though Caw was sure he had never heard it before.

"Those who talk to animals," said Crumb. "I believe you've met three others already, though there are many more."

"The prisoners," said Caw.

"Of course!" said Lydia. "The dogs, the cockroaches. And that hideous snake!"

"Lydia?" said Mr. Strickham. "Sweetheart, please come down."

Her face twisted with anger, and she leaned over the edge of the platform. "You lied to me!" she shouted. "You said you'd let me talk to him."

"The time for talking is over," said Mr. Strickham. "Get down here at once!"

What now? said Screech. *Last stand?*

"The police can't stop those bad ferals," said Crumb. "Listen to me, crow talker. There's another way out of here."

"How?" said Lydia, throwing up her hands and casting a look around the confines of the nest. "Fly?"

Crumb shot her a glance. "Yes," he said simply.

Lydia rolled her eyes, but Crumb wasn't smiling.

"I'm serious," he said. He looked at Caw, his blue eyes alive. "Get your crows to carry you."

Caw gestured to Milky, Screech, and Glum. "There are only three of them," he said. "They can't possibly lift me."

"So call more," said Crumb, with a frustrated shake of his head. "Come on!"

"I . . . I can't," said Caw. "I don't know how."

Crumb gripped him hard on the arm. "Have you ever tried?" he said, leaning close enough for Caw to see the chip in his front tooth.

With his free hand, Crumb tore the tarpaulin from half of the nest, letting in the daylight. "Watch and learn," he said.

Crumb raised both arms and whistled. Within seconds, black spots appeared in the sky to the east. Pigeons—hundreds of them! Caw stared openmouthed as the flock crossed the park toward them, then swooped low over the treetops and landed, one by one, on Crumb's arms and shoulders.

"What's going on up there?" shouted Mr. Strickham.

As more and more birds arrived, Caw saw that Lydia was gaping just like him. It was the strangest sight he had ever seen, but familiar too. His dream—the night at his bedroom window when the crows had come and taken him. It was just like this.

"Where've they come from?" said someone from below.

Caw glanced down and spotted an officer in a trench coat next to Mr. Strickham, giving silent commands with his hands to the other policemen. They were pressing closer to the bottom of the tree.

"Now you try!" said Crumb. The pigeons flapped and warbled as they jostled for position over his body.

"It won't work," said Caw, his heart hammering in his chest.

"Do it!" said Crumb fiercely.

With the tarpaulin pulled back, Caw stood tall in the nest. Lydia was watching him, an intense gleam in her eyes.

"Go on," she said, nodding encouragement. "You can do it. I know you can."

Caw reached out his arms.

"*Will* them to come!" said Crumb.

Caw tried a whistle like the older man had done, and his three crows jumped up onto his arm. For once, neither Screech nor Glum spoke a word. Caw saw that they wore a strange, vacant expression, almost as if a trance had descended over them. He closed his eyes. *Come to me!* he urged. *Come to me!*

"That's right," said Crumb. "You're doing it!"

Caw clenched his fists and imagined power in his arms. He imagined himself drawing the birds toward him. He opened one eye and saw that in the distance, over the prison, birds had gathered.

"That's amazing!" whispered Lydia.

Caw focused on the feeling. And then he didn't have to imagine it anymore, because it was really happening. Not just in his arms. He felt a ball of warmth in the pit of his stomach, growing and swelling until it spread through his limbs, right to his fingertips and beyond. Half a dozen crows alighted on his arms, birds he was sure he'd never seen before. Caw closed his eyes again as the energy gripped him, making him feel light, as though his body weighed little more than a feather. He felt countless crows, their talons scrabbling at his jacket. Each bird that landed made him stronger than before. Stronger and lighter.

Caw realized he couldn't feel the nest beneath his feet anymore and opened his eyes. He was floating, as the crows flapped their wings in time. His memory from all those years ago at the window returned, fresher than ever. But this wasn't the same at all. Then he had felt only fear and confusion. Now he felt in control. He could sense the crows' beating wings as if they were part of him.

"I'd grab on if I were you," said Crumb to Lydia. Caw noticed Crumb's heels were no longer touching the nest either. He was suspended a foot . . . no, a yard. . . above the timber planks.

"Are you serious?" Lydia asked.

"Hold on," said Caw, never more sure of his words. Lydia wrapped her arms around his middle. A part of his brain acknowledged that no one had hugged him like this for as long as he could remember, but it didn't feel awkward—it felt warm, powerful. It gave him even more strength.

"We're coming up!" said Mr. Strickham, his voice panicky. "If you hurt my daughter, Caw . . ."

"Ready to go?" asked Crumb, landing on the very edge of the nest. "On the count of three, we jump! Trust the birds, Caw, and they won't fail you."

I trust them, thought Caw.

He set his feet down beside Crumb's, just as a policeman's head poked through the hatch.

"One . . ."

The cop turned toward them and his mouth dropped open. A hundred crows screeched and squawked in protest.

"Go!" said Lydia. "Quickly!"

"Two . . ."

Caw looked down through the branches. The fall would kill them, without a doubt. But he wouldn't fall. He couldn't.

"Three!" said Crumb.

The policeman lunged forward as Caw stepped off into nothingness.

10

A scream split the air, and Caw realized it was his own. He was plummeting downward. Lydia's arms dug tight into his sides.

And then all of a sudden they weren't falling anymore. Caw's legs wheeled in the empty air, and his stomach settled back to where it belonged. A gun went off with a crack, and he heard the soft *phut* of a bullet hitting wood.

"Hold your fire!" shouted Mr. Strickham. "Lydia!"

Caw saw the branches of the tree sinking below them at a sickening pace as Lydia's father and the policemen stared upward in astonishment. With every foot the crows climbed, Caw felt smaller, his body more fragile.

"This can't be happening!" murmured Lydia, clinging to him tightly.

Caw glanced across and saw Crumb hanging from his pigeons. He must have weighed twice as much as Caw, but the pigeons seemed to be having no trouble. They turned as one and flew in the direction of the park gates, Crumb a raggedy scarecrow in their grip. Behind Caw the police became dots as the circular pond passed below like a dirty copper coin.

A laugh of pure delight escaped his lips.

"Caw, I can't believe this," Lydia said, breathless with excitement.

The crows' wing beats were smooth and steady. As Caw's fear melted away, he could feel his racing heartbeat slow to match their rhythm. Lydia was right—this *couldn't* be happening. It defied all laws of physics and gravity. It was . . . *magic*.

They gathered speed and the wind buffeted their bodies. They crossed the railway tracks, flying above the smoking factories and then the northern curve of the Blackwater. From the sky, the river looked like a snake coiling through the city. A few boats scarred its dark surface with white wakes. Caw gazed in wonder at the city's vastness reduced to a grid of streets and a patchwork of rooftops. He saw the library, small enough to reach out and pluck from the ground. Beyond, the edges of the city came into view, borders he'd never dreamed he would see. Pastures of beige and green spread all the way to the horizon, interspersed with huge, scattered expanses of dark forest.

Lydia clung to him, her feet resting on his. Her hair whipped around his face and she looked up at him, grinning, though her lips were going blue with cold. He felt a rush of guilt. He should never have doubted her.

Crumb's pigeons wheeled west toward the sun and dipped their flight. Caw willed his crows to follow and they did, leveling their wings into a glide. The sun warmed his face as the wind rushed through his hair. They crossed the Blackwater again, and he saw a train threading over the railway bridge. They were too high to hear the thunderous roar of its engines.

They were heading for a church, he realized, its spire piercing the sky like a dagger. The building was surrounded by ruined low-rise buildings. They swooped low, right across a parking lot, toward the huge church door.

The ground rushed up, and Caw felt a sudden surge of panic. A few of the crows let go, and he dropped several feet as the remainder adjusted to take their weight. He drew up his legs instinctively. But the crows banked as one, tipping back their wings. A yard or so above the ground, their talons released him.

Lydia screamed and lost her grip, hitting the ground and rolling over. Caw lost sight of her as he slammed down. Unable to stay on his feet, he tucked up his elbows and tumbled over on his side, pain shooting through his limbs.

When he came to a halt, bruised and shaken, he saw the crows scattering through the sky like flakes of ash in the wind. All except Milky, Glum, and Screech. "Thank you," Caw whispered.

Crumb alighted in front of them, landing softly on his feet. He took a handful of seeds from his pocket and scattered them on the ground, sending his pigeons into a frenzy of pecking. It was hard to imagine that a few moments ago they'd been carrying a fully grown human through the air. Crumb grinned mischievously. "I should have said, landing's tricky to master."

Lydia was first to her feet and pulled Caw up. "Well, that was different," she said.

Caw nodded, staring at Milky, Screech, and Glum. "I'm learning a few things too," he said quietly.

"Welcome to chez Crumb," said Crumb, gesturing toward the hulking building. "Or the Church of St. Francis, as she was once known."

"You *live* here?" said Lydia.

The church might have been grand once—like many of the others in Blackstone—but it had obviously been badly damaged by fire. The stonework was blackened in large swathes, and half the roof slates were gone, leaving charred timberwork open to the elements like an exposed rib cage. It made Caw think of a decomposing creature, pecked at by scavengers.

"We can't all have feather beds and running water," said Crumb, his lips drooping momentarily before the smile reasserted itself. "Come on in."

The pigeons peeled off the ground and flapped through the gaping hole in the roof, settling on the lofty beams.

"Don't need to worry about security around here," said Crumb, as he pushed open the doors with both hands. Caw and Lydia followed.

Inside, the church was a wreck. The stonework was covered in graffiti, and not a single one of the filthy windows was intact. It smelled damp and forgotten, with something more pungent in the air that caught the back of Caw's throat. Pews were scattered at angles on the floor. There had once been a cross on the wall at the far end, but all that remained was a slightly paler section of stone. Caw wondered if it had been rescued when the building caught fire or had simply been stolen.

Taking two steps at a time with his long strides, Crumb led them up a narrow stone spiral staircase. Lydia came after Caw, with the crows' talons scrabbling on the stone as they hopped up at the rear. A chill draft cooled the air.

"This whole district was gutted by fire during the Dark Summer," said Crumb. "The city had no money to rebuild it, so the area was pretty much abandoned."

A low doorway at the top opened onto another level at the back end of the church. The floor was gone in patches, exposing rafters beneath the floorboards. More pigeons gathered at the far end, around what looked like glowing embers in an old tin drum. The boy with dirty-blond hair who Caw had seen in the alley with Crumb sat beside it, stirring something in a pot. He looked up and flashed a smile as they approached.

"How's dinner coming, Pip?" called Crumb.

"Who's she?" asked Pip, nodding at Lydia.

"My *name* is Lydia," she said. "And who are you?"

Pip ignored her and turned back to the pot. "You took your time," he said.

Crumb strode across the floorboards. "No need to be rude to our guests," he said. "We had some trouble with the police. Had to make an aerial getaway."

"They see you?" said Pip, shooting them an urgent look.

"I'm afraid so," said Crumb. "We had little choice in the matter." He looked to Caw and Lydia. "You hungry? Pip's been cooking his specialty—pumpkin soup."

Caw was about to follow, when he noticed that Lydia was staring out a broken window, a worried look on her face. "Are you okay?" he asked her.

"Oh—yeah," she said. "I'm fine." She paused a moment. "I was just thinking about my mom and dad. They'll probably ground me for life for this."

Caw looked at the floor. "If you want, I can find a way to get you back—"

"No!" Lydia cut him off. "I was just carried across the city by a flock of birds. *Birds.* I'm not going home until I know everything."

Without another word, Lydia hurried after Crumb. Caw followed.

They settled onto the floor around the brazier. The sun was low in the sky, and Crumb went around with a box of matches, lighting a few candles planted into old wine bottles.

"So you're a *feral*," said Lydia, looking first at Crumb, then at Caw. "You both are!"

Crumb held the match in front of his face, and his features were cast in shade and orange light. His eyes, for a moment, looked a lot older than the rest of him. He blew the match out. "Yes," he said. "And Pip here."

Crumb held chipped mugs while Pip ladled in the soup. Steam rose off it, and a draft whipped the gray wisps away through the roof. Dusk was falling, and all was quiet apart from the occasional warble of a pigeon. Caw sipped the delicious thick soup as Crumb began to speak.

"Blackstone is no ordinary city, you see," said Crumb. "There's something special about it. No one knows what exactly, but the fact is, this place attracts people like us. There used to be more ferals here—the ones who have the gift and can talk to animals. Now only a few remain."

Caw felt like he'd waited his entire life to hear this.

"So Caw's a bird feral?" said Lydia, leaning forward.

"Just crows," said Crumb, flashing her a fierce look. "The pigeons, they're mine." His tone softened. "But it's not always birds. . . ."

Pip snapped his fingers, and two mice poked their twitching noses from his coat pocket.

"Cool!" said Lydia.

Pip blushed. "You can stroke them," he said. "These two don't nip."

Lydia reached forward to pet them, and the mice chirruped happily.

"So Jawbone, Mamba, and Scuttle—they're ferals too," said Caw.

"Powerful ones," said Crumb, his face somber. "And evil." He tipped the last of his soup down his throat. When he set down his mug, Caw saw some drops in his beard. Crumb wiped his chin with the back of his sleeve.

"Where are the others?" said Caw.

"All over the city," said Crumb. "Some I know of, some I don't. A long, long time ago, ordinary people knew all about ferals. They let us be, living in harmony with the natural world. But then things changed. It started with accusations of witchcraft and sorcery. A few ferals were rooted out. Others went into hiding, but some fought back, and that only made the problem worse. Many feral lines were . . . ended. After that, the survivors learned to keep their powers a secret. Their gift became a curse."

"Feral 'lines,'" said Caw. "What do you mean?"

Crumb helped himself to more pumpkin soup. "A feral's powers come from their mother or father," he said. "When the parent feral dies, the gift passes on to the eldest child."

The room seemed to dim. Caw's mind stirred and focused. "So one of my parents . . ."

Crumb cocked his head. "You really don't know?"

"Know what?" said Caw.

After a pause, Crumb spoke again. "It was your mother," he said. "She was the crow talker before you."

Caw let the words sink in. If what Crumb was saying was true, it could only mean one thing. "But I have the powers now, so she must be . . ."

Crumb and Pip shared a glance, and then Crumb nodded solemnly. He placed a hand on Caw's shoulder. "I'm sorry. Your mother died a long time ago. I thought you knew."

Caw looked at the mug in his hands, so they couldn't see the tears misting in his eyes. "I guess I did," he said. But he'd always hoped, all these years. That one day she would come and get him.

"She was a brave woman," said Crumb. "Impressive."

Caw's heart lurched. "You knew her?"

Crumb shook his head. "No, but I saw her a couple of times when I was young. I didn't even dare to say hello."

Questions flocked into Caw's mind. He stared at his crows. Only Milky was looking his way, blind and direct at the same time. Screech and Glum had averted their gaze.

"You knew too, didn't you?" he said quietly to the crows. Suddenly it made sense—the crows carrying him away in his memory. His mother had commanded them to, just like he had commanded them himself today. "You *must* have known," he repeated, louder. He couldn't stop the tears rolling anymore. Lydia looked at him sadly.

Finally Glum lifted his beak. *We heard,* he said. *The story passed on to us. Years passed too. It never seemed the right time to tell you. We were doing fine, and you were safe.*

"But . . ." Caw sniffed and fought back the tears. "But you could have told me. All this time, I never understood. I thought they *abandoned* me, Glum."

They sent you away for your own safety, said Glum. He *came for them.*

The room felt suddenly ten degrees colder. An image burned into his brain, bold and terrifying at the edge of his mind. A body marked with an *M*, and eight creeping legs . . .

"The spider feral," he said.

It was Crumb's turn to look surprised. "How could you—"

"He was in a dream I have," said Caw. "I think he had something to do with Miss Wallace being killed, too." He swallowed, sickened by guilt.

"The woman at the library?" said Crumb.

Caw told Crumb what he had seen—the graffiti outside the fire exit and the mesh of webbing over the librarian's mouth.

Crumb's face was ashen pale beneath all the dirt. Pip, Caw noticed, was shaking. "Jawbone and the others," said Crumb. "They were his followers when he was alive. But painting his mark now . . ."

"What do they want?" asked Lydia.

Crumb shifted a little. "Good ferals work in harmony with their animals," he said, "but bad ones force their will. The spider feral was the worst. He called himself the Spinning Man."

Something clicked in Caw's brain when he heard the name. Lydia in the library, sketching out the picture of the spider. She had said that the spider's body was shaped like an *S*, and in the middle of it, the spiky *M* shape. *The Spinning Man.*

Caw shivered. "Tell us everything."

Crumb went on. "The Spinning Man wasn't content to stay hidden among normal humans. He wanted power. So he gathered other renegade ferals and tried to take over the city. It happened eight years ago."

"The Dark Summer!" said Lydia.

Crumb shuddered visibly. "I wasn't much older than you are now. He made it his mission to find all the good ferals and . . . and wipe them out. He almost managed it, too. Perhaps your mother suspected he was coming for her. If the Spinning Man had found out about your existence, he would have killed you as well as them."

"What about my father?" said Caw.

"He was found with her," said Crumb. "He stood by her and . . . and he paid the price."

"Oh, Caw," said Lydia in a whisper. "I'm so sorry." She slipped her hand into his and squeezed it tight.

Caw felt utterly drained. The hope that his parents were somehow alive had been snuffed out for good. Each revelation threw new, painful light on the past. Suddenly his parents weren't just figures dimly imagined in a dream, faces fading to nothing as the crows carried him away. They were real people who had loved him and who had given their lives to save him. Caw's heart felt ready to burst.

"The history books say the Dark Summer ended abruptly," Crumb went on. "The truth is that the Spinning Man was killed. That's what finally put a stop to the bloodshed." He suddenly sat up straighter, and his face hardened as he glared into the fire of the brazier. "We fought with everything we had—those who remained—and at last one of our number killed him. It took all our strength, and many died." His eyes seemed to be staring right through the flames.

"Of course, the authorities in Blackstone just called it a crime wave. They blamed it on mass hysteria. Without their leader to guide them, the Spinning Man's followers became careless—the Blackstone police managed to catch a lot of them. Others fled and went into hiding. Peace returned, until now. . . ."

"Hang on a minute," said Lydia. "You said the good ferals *killed* the Spinning Man. But then why are his followers still using his symbol? What about the graffiti? What does it all mean?"

"He *is* dead, isn't he?" asked Pip. He suddenly sounded very young indeed.

"Oh, he's dead," Crumb replied, "but . . ."

"But what?" said Lydia.

At his side, Caw spotted Milky looking agitated, ruffling his feathers.

"I've seen the Spinning Man's symbol too," said Crumb. "Scratched on a park bench. Sprayed on a car hood. Scrawled on the wall of a warehouse near the river. His followers must be gathering again. That's why we ran into you behind the restaurant, Caw— we've been out watching the city, making sure our old friends are safe. Now I'm sure they're not—none of us are." He paused. "I've had strange dreams, just like you, Caw. Dreams of spiders. I'm not sure why."

Caw sensed he wasn't telling them something—something important. "But you have an idea, don't you?"

Crumb stood up and walked away from the brazier, silhouetted against the darkening sky. He stood at the edge of the floorboards and looked across to his roosting pigeons, deep in thought. After half a minute of silence, he turned back toward them. "It's not as simple as it seems—life and death."

"Yes, it is," said Lydia. "You're either alive, or you're dead." She looked across at Caw, her face in shadow from the brazier. Her eyes shone fearfully.

"Perhaps," said Crumb. "I hope so."

Caw thought about his parents, killed by the Spinning Man and his followers. Anger flooded his body. If he couldn't have revenge on the spider feral himself, Jawbone, Scuttle, and Mamba were still at large. They had to pay.

"We need to stop them!" he said. "We have to fight back."

"They belong in prison," said Lydia.

Pip giggled, breaking the tense atmosphere. The mouse feral clamped a hand over his mouth.

"What's so funny?" demanded Caw.

"Nothing," said Pip. "It's just . . . well, you haven't got a chance."

"What do you mean?" Caw hated the smirk on the younger boy's face.

"Pip . . . ," said Crumb in a warning voice.

"No." Pip's tone was defiant. "I've been watching you, Caw. You skulk around the park, barely scraping enough to eat. You hardly ever dare come down from that nest. You live with three raggedy crows. . . ."

Hey! squawked Screech and Glum.

"I'm tougher than you think," said Caw, standing over Pip.

"Pip's right," said Crumb matter-of-factly. "You can't control your powers."

"I rescued Lydia and her dad," said Caw. "Jawbone was going to kill them!"

"And his crows got us away from the police at the library," said Lydia.

Crumb nodded. "You've got guts, I'll give you that," he said. "But against other ferals with all their animals? What if Jawbone had a whole pack of dogs with him? Or what if Mamba summoned a dozen snakes instead of one? You're lucky we saved you when we did. Our best bet now is to stay hidden."

Caw remembered his terror in the library, pinned by a slavering monster of a dog and completely defenseless. He felt his confidence seep away.

"You're right," he said.

"No, he's not, Caw," said Lydia firmly. "You chased the snake from my house too. Don't give up."

Crumb cocked his head, looking at Lydia with a frown. "You remind me of someone I once knew," he said. "Someone very brave indeed."

"I bet he didn't give up, did he?" said Lydia.

Crumb shook his head. "No, *she* did not."

Lydia's encouragement fired Caw's heart. "Well, let's fight then," he said. "I summoned a whole flock today. I can learn."

"Not fast enough," said Crumb. "They'd kill you, Caw. Just like your mother."

The words cut deep. "Let me try!"

Crumb and Pip looked at each other, and Pip shrugged.

"Listen," said Crumb. "Let me show you what you're facing. You and I—we'll have a duel—a contest of powers. I've had a dozen years of practice, and I wouldn't stand a chance against Jawbone, Scuttle, or Mamba. When you see how easily I beat you, perhaps you'll reconsider."

"A duel?" said Caw.

"This is going to be funny," said Pip.

Caw's lip twisted into a snarl. *They're laughing at me,* he thought.

"You can do it!" said Lydia, slapping him hard on the shoulder.

Caw felt Milky's blind gaze on his face, and in that moment he knew he wouldn't back down.

"You're on," he said.

11

Caw stood with his back to the entrance, staring down the central aisle of the church.

You sure about this? said Screech. The crows were perched on a pew nearby.

"No," muttered Caw, "but I've got to try."

Crumb sat at the front of the church, under the white outline of the missing cross. He slouched on the bare altar table, legs dangling over the side. "Ready?" called the pigeon talker.

"Come on, Caw!" shouted Lydia from the gallery above.

"Teach him a lesson, Crumb," yelled Pip from beside her.

"I'm ready," said Caw.

Crumb whistled like he had at the nest, and there was a bustle of beating wings as hundreds of pigeons descended from the roof beams and landed around his feet.

Okay, that was impressive, said Glum, tilting his head.

I can't look, said Screech, shielding his eyes beneath a wing.

Caw stretched out his arms and willed the crows to come. He felt the same warmth building in the pit of his stomach as he'd felt earlier. He could do this.

Crumb flung out his left arm, and all the pigeons on that side took flight at once, their wings cracking like whips. They flew straight at Caw.

Caw's concentration broke into panic. "Stop them!" he yelled.

Geronimo! cried Screech.

The three crows took to the air, but the pigeons swamped them in seconds. Amid the melee of feathers and squawks, Milky, Screech, and Glum were completely outnumbered. The pigeons forced them to the ground, and Pip's high-pitched laugher filled the nave.

"That's not fair!" said Lydia. "Caw didn't have time to call his crows."

Crumb was still seated on the altar table, looking very relaxed indeed.

"You think the Spinning Man's followers will give Caw time?" he said. "You're lucky it's only a few friendly pigeons. Jawbone's dogs would have torn those three crows to pieces."

The crows continued to struggle helplessly against the weight of pigeons. Caw wanted to run and kick the vermin birds away, but he knew that would be giving up. Instead he forced himself to concentrate, to draw the crows to him once more.

"Sorry about this," said Crumb, standing up from the altar table and brushing his hands together like the fight was over. "But now you can see . . ."

Caw felt power swelling in his gut. He sensed the crows gathering. *They're coming,* he thought with a smile.

The door burst open with a bang, and Caw felt a rush of triumph at the shock on Crumb's face. The older feral jerked to his feet as dozens of black shapes swooped past Caw and straight toward the carpet of pigeons. Caw waited until his birds reached Crumb's, then threw his arm toward Crumb. The crows steered in a dark wave to attack the pigeon talker, their wings snapping up and down.

"Go, Caw!" shouted Lydia.

"Look out!" said Pip.

Crumb clapped his hands together, and his remaining pigeons flew in a tight crisscross formation in front of him. Crumb disappeared completely behind the curtain of gray.

The crow attack parted the sea of pigeons straight through the middle, scattering them in all directions.

Then the pigeons dropped as one to the ground.

Crumb had vanished.

"What?" said Caw.

"Just a trick of the trade," said Crumb's voice in his ear.

Caw spun around to find the pigeon talker standing on the pew beside him.

"How did you do that?" he said.

"A little sleight of hand goes a long way," said Crumb. He pulled apart his coat, and a dozen pigeons burst from inside. They swamped

Caw, pecking and clawing, driving him along the pew until he hit the stone wall and couldn't go any farther. Their shrieks were so shrill he struggled to think. His arms flailed as he tried to cover his face and drive them off, but there were too many. He wanted to summon his crows, but he couldn't even open his eyes to look for them. The world had shrunk to flapping wings and screaming birds and stinging scratches wherever his skin was exposed.

"Please," he yelled. "Please, make them stop!"

In a heartbeat the pigeon attack ceased. Caw slumped against the wall, ashamed, as the pigeons flew back into the rafters. The other crows had gone, leaving only his three loyal companions perched on the pew, looking ruffled but uninjured.

"Woo-hoo!" cried Pip. "Crumb wins!"

Crumb walked over and offered Caw his hand. "Forgive me," he said. "I shouldn't have started showing off."

Caw could hardly look the pigeon talker in the eye, but he let himself be pulled upright. His hands and forearms were bleeding, but none of the scratches were deep.

Good try, Caw, said Screech.

A for effort, Glum added with a heavy hint of sarcasm.

Screech butted up against the older crow's side. *He did his best.*

Caw snorted. "But my best was nowhere near good enough," he said. Looking up, he saw Lydia staring at him, her eyes full of sympathy.

"No, it wasn't," said Crumb simply. "If you went up against the Spinning Man's followers now, you would be dead, and so would your crows, and your feral line would be no more."

Caw looked at Screech, Milky, and Glum. They'd die for him, he realized, but they were only three birds. And however many he managed to call today still wasn't enough.

"How do you summon so many?" he asked Crumb.

"Willpower," said the pigeon talker. "And a lot of practice. I've been a feral for much longer than you, and I've always known the threats we face."

"Then teach me," said Caw.

"It would take months," said Crumb. "No, *years* of intense training. There isn't time."

"I could learn quickly," said Caw, trying to sound more confident than he felt.

Crumb smiled. "Even if you could, you're not a fighter, Caw. The people we'd be up against—they're brutal. They don't have any mercy."

Lydia and Pip joined them at the bottom of the stairs. Lydia's lips were pressed in a determined line.

"We can't give up," said Caw. "We can't just hide away!"

"Can't we?" said Crumb. "Stay here, with us. We'll be safe."

"They'll find us," Lydia told Crumb, her voice hard. For a moment it felt to Caw like she was the adult, and Crumb the child.

"And how do you know that?" said Crumb defensively. "Pip and

I have never been bothered here before."

Lydia huffed. "Maybe that's because no one's come *looking* for you before. There are three of them out there. And who knows—they may join up with others too. You might be able to hide for a while, but it will only take one slipup, and they'll strike."

Silence fell in the church. Caw felt completely powerless.

"There were stories once," Crumb murmured. "Stories of ferals so powerful they could *become* the animals they controlled."

"Just stories?" said Caw.

"Well, I've never met one," said Crumb. "I've been training since I was fifteen and I haven't come close."

"Maybe you just don't know how?" said Lydia, tipping her chin up in challenge.

"Listen, you!" Crumb said, his face flushed with anger. "You don't know anything about this. You haven't lost friends and loved ones, or creatures as dear to you as family."

"I have, actually," said Lydia. For a moment her bold expression dropped. "Mamba's snake killed my dog, Benjy. He was my best friend in the world."

Crumb stared at her, his gaze softening. "I'm sorry to hear that," he said quietly. "But the point still stands. We don't have a hope this time."

"We have to at least try," said Caw.

"And get killed?" said Pip. "What's the point in that?"

"We'll die anyway if they hunt us down," said Caw.

"And they know where I live," Lydia interrupted. "They know where my *family* lives."

"It's true," said Caw. "If you won't help us, Lydia and I will go against them alone."

We'll come too! said Screech, hopping along the back of the pew.

Will we? said Glum, looking askance at the younger crow. He shrugged his wings. *I suppose we have to.*

Caw grabbed Lydia's hand and walked toward the church door.

"Listen to you!" Pip called after them. "The boy who can barely control three crows. Now you're talking like you're Felix Quaker with lives to spare!"

Caw froze. *Quaker.* He felt Lydia tighten her grip on his hand.

"Who's Felix Quaker?" he said, turning around.

Crumb shrugged. "The cat feral," he said. "He's rumored to have nine lives—and to have been around for a couple of hundred years."

Caw glanced at Lydia. "We need to talk to him."

Crumb shook his head. "You won't get any help from old Quaker. He's not exactly friendly. He sat out the Dark Summer—locked himself away in his mansion—and wouldn't join either side."

"But he's in Blackstone?" said Caw.

"Yes," said Crumb. "Lives in Gort House. Great big place on Herrick Hill—spires and turrets and the rest. He collects anything to do with feral lore. Memorabilia, books, all kinds of junk. And he knows more feral history than most people can be bothered to remember."

"I know the place!" said Lydia. "Everyone says the guy who lives there is crazy."

"Not far off, if you want my opinion," said Crumb.

"But maybe he can help us," said Caw eagerly.

"He's not fond of visitors," said Crumb, shaking his head. "You're better off focusing on your skills, learning to defend yourself and keeping from getting caught."

Lydia was watching Caw, frowning slightly. He knew what she was thinking: *Why aren't you telling him about Miss Wallace's note?*

He shrugged at her, hoping Crumb wouldn't notice. Why should he tell the pigeon talker *everything*? Okay, Crumb had given them shelter, but that was as far as it went. Caw was sure that more answers lay with this cat feral, perched on his hill above the river. He was tired of the surprises, and tired of people telling him what to do—he wanted to be in charge for once.

Crumb sighed. "Look, why don't you stay the night? Lie low until morning, and then we can talk again."

Caw nodded in agreement. But secretly, he was already making other plans.

Caw is dreaming.

It's the same dream as before, only now he is watching as the tall, pale stranger brings down the knocker of his parents' house. The moonlight glints on his spider ring.

"Don't answer it," Caw shouts, but no sound escapes his lips. The door opens of its own accord.

This is the horror his crows carried him away from. But now, for the first time, they bring him inside, in the wake of the stranger.

In the wake of the Spinning Man.

The door slams closed behind them.

Caw sees his parents, standing side by side in front of a dining-room table. Two half-empty glasses of wine sit there. A single crow perches on the floor at their feet. Caw's mother faces the Spinning Man, unflinching, the folds of her black dress billowing around her like a crow's wings, as though she controls the very air around her.

"Get out of my house," she commands through gritted teeth. Caw can see sweat glistening on her forehead, as if she were straining with effort. "I'm not telling you where it is." The crow puffs up its feathers in agreement.

"Don't come any closer!" shouts Caw's father. He's standing next to his wife, brandishing a poker from the fireplace.

The Spinning Man just smiles. "And what are you planning to do with that?" he asks, his voice like silk drawn over stones. He nods at the poker.

Caw's mother looks at her husband. "Please, you have to get out of here. Now. This is nothing to do with you."

"I'm not leaving you," he tells her.

"I can handle that monster," Caw's mother says, her eyes focused on the Spinning Man. But her voice sounds tired.

"I think not," says the Spinning Man. "Not without your crows."

With horror, Caw sees that the windows are open but covered in a pale gauze: spiderwebs. Listening closely, he can hear the wing beats and desperate cries of hundreds of crows trying to break through.

"If you won't tell me what I want to know, then you're of no more use to me, crow talker."

Caw's mother falters—her dress hangs loose around her now. She turns to her husband and says, "Run, darling—please, just run."

"No," Caw's father says, grasping her hand in his. "Never."

"As you wish," says the Spinning Man. "You can die together."

He lifts a hand, and the room darkens as though he's dimmed the lights.

From the corners shadows begin to crawl. Not shadows—spiders. Hundreds of them. They emerge from the ceiling too, descending the walls like falling drapes of black. The crow tries to take off but is overwhelmed by crawling creatures. Caw's parents press closer to each other and back into the table. A glass of wine smashes onto the floor. Caw wants to rush forward, but the crows hold him, a powerless spectator. There are thousands of spiders now, their legs shuffling as one. They close on his parents, a carpet of glistening black bodies. So many that he can hear the rustle and chatter of their movements.

Caw watches as the spiders crawl over his parents' feet and up their legs. They try to brush them away, but there are too many. The poker falls, landing among the spiders with a soft thud. Caw's parents squirm and writhe like they're on fire as the spiders consume them, and he feels their agony in his own powerlessness. The sounds from their mouths are not cries of pain, but worse. Short, panicked wails. The spiders cross their chests, their shoulders, and their necks.

Caw wants to look away, but he can't.

Now they're straining their chins upward, as if they're drowning, searching for air. His father howls, and then chokes as spiders pour into his mouth.

With her last breath, Caw's mother speaks to the Spinning Man in a muffled voice. "You won't win. You'll see." A moment later, the spiders silence her. Her eyes find Caw at last, and a wind seems to rush out of her, whirling toward him like a gale. It lasts for a split second before the tide of spider legs blinds her and . . .

Caw woke with a gasp. The church attic swam into focus, lit only by the glowing embers of the fire in the brazier. He propped himself up on his elbow, shivering under the threadbare blanket. The dream still held him in its clutches, wringing his nerves. He pressed his eyes shut, trying to stamp out the nightmare images.

Was that really how they had died, in wordless terror, choked by the Spinning Man's creatures? Milky landed silently beside him and cocked his head. His pale eyes were moist. In that moment, Caw knew it was the truth.

Crumb was on his back, a whistling sound escaping his lips with every breath. Pip was huddled under blankets, completely hidden. Across the rafters, an army of pigeons had their beaks tucked into the thick feathers of their breasts.

If Caw was going to slip away, now was the time.

12

As slowly and smoothly as he could, Caw pushed the blanket off and rose into a sitting position. Lydia was facing the other way, fast asleep. He had been planning to wake her, but the dream had changed his mind. If the prisoners were followers of the Spinning Man—that nightmarish creature—she was better off as far away from Caw as possible. With any luck, Crumb would help her get home.

As soon as he stood up, Screech and Glum began to twitch on their perches near the stairwell. Caw put his finger to his lips and they remained silent, watching him inquisitively. He pulled on his coat and tiptoed across the floorboards. Then he padded down the steps, followed by his crows.

Don't suppose we're going back to the nest, said Screech, shivering as Caw unlatched the church door.

"Not yet," whispered Caw.

Outside, he took a last look at the silent church. He wondered what it had been like before the Dark Summer. A place of happiness, probably, where families and friends gathered together in peace. But the Spinning Man had destroyed all that.

The dream spiders crept into his mind again, their gleaming bodies twitching, their footfalls light and quiet as scattered pins. He shuddered and forced the memory away.

Caw crept across the deserted parking lot, savoring the silent cold of the night. He was just turning onto the road toward the river when he heard footsteps rushing up behind him.

We've got company, said Glum, passing overhead. Caw raised his hands to defend himself as he twisted around.

It was Lydia. Her face was pale, and she looked as though she hadn't slept a wink. "You're going to find Quaker, aren't you?" she said. "Well, I'm coming too."

Caw lowered his hands and sighed. "You don't have to," he told her.

"I know. But I want to. Those prisoners threatened my family too, remember?"

"Don't suppose I can really stop you, can I?" he said, raising his eyebrows.

Lydia grinned. "I'll take that as an invitation."

You would, muttered Glum. He flew upward and away.

They set off together, over the steel girders of a railway bridge spanning the Blackwater. At this time of night there were no trains rumbling across.

"You've got good hearing," said Caw. "Even the pigeons didn't wake up."

"I must get it from my mom. She *always* hears me listening to music when I should be doing homework. Even when I've got my headphones on!"

Caw grinned. After being so sure he should leave her behind, he was pleased she was here. With Lydia and the crows at his side, he felt more confident. His parents had done all they could to protect him, so that the crow feral line could continue. He was going to make sure they hadn't died in vain.

"Your parents sound like they were very brave," said Lydia, as if she could read his thoughts. They had reached the other side of the river. "You must be proud."

"I guess so," said Caw as they began to walk along the north bank. Arches lined the embankment, shops and stalls all shuttered up for the night.

His latest dream was an ever-present shadow, and his parents' cries as the spiders overwhelmed them seemed like faded echoes. He didn't feel ready to tell Lydia about it, not with the terror still so fresh. All his life he had let his bitterness toward them grow, but now it seemed as though that anger was misplaced. It was the Spinning Man who deserved his rage—for taking his parents away from him.

"I hope *my* mom and dad are okay," said Lydia quietly.

"Me too," said Caw automatically.

"They're not bad people, you know," said Lydia.

Caw looked sideways at her.

"I know they haven't been very nice to you," she added.

"Do you mean when they locked me in a room, or when your dad tried to arrest me?" said Caw, trying to keep a straight face.

Lydia giggled. "Yes, but you'll see. When all this is over and the prisoners are back behind bars, they'll get to know you properly. You can come for dinner again!"

"That didn't go very well, did it?" said Caw. Despite everything, he was smiling at the memory. "I must have looked like an animal."

Lydia suddenly slowed her steps, then sped up again. Her eyes were fixed resolutely ahead.

"What?" said Caw.

"Nothing," said Lydia. "Let's hurry."

Caw stopped and looked around. Then his eyes fell on a stack of newspapers, tied with a cord, sitting on the pavement outside a closed newspaper stand. The front page was dominated by a picture of his face.

"Oh, no," he said. He walked over to it, sinking to his knees beside the stack.

Good likeness, said Screech, hopping onto one corner.

It wasn't perfect—just a drawing in black and white—but it was good enough. Beneath were several words in huge writing and two much smaller pictures—photographs—of Lydia and Miss Wallace. "What does it say?" he asked.

Lydia looked over his shoulder. "You don't want to know."

"Tell me!" said Caw.

"It says you're wanted for questioning about the murder."

Caw squeezed his eyes shut. "What am I going to do now? The whole city will be looking for me."

Lydia touched his arm. "Those people just want to sell papers, Caw," she said. "We'll set them straight. And when all this is over . . ."

"I know, I know," he said with a touch of irritation. "Everything will be back to the way it was."

He tugged up his collar and set off again, with Lydia trotting behind. He knew she was only trying to comfort him, but deep down he was sure that *nothing* would ever be normal again. He was walking a path with no way back. At the end lay either the truth and revenge, or the same fate that his parents had met.

The spider this way crawls, Milky had said. *And we are but prey in his web.*

The crows circled over the river and above their heads. Though it was well after midnight, the streets weren't quite empty. Occasional cars swished past, and drunk people spilled out of bars. Caw kept his head down as they headed to the west of the city. The gates of Blackstone Zoo were locked, but Caw could smell the creatures and the warmth of their sleeping bodies. He had never been inside, but the crows had told him of all the animals in their cages, and even taught him their names using a picture book back at the nest. *Is there a feral for each and every creature?* he wondered. Crumb had said there were lots more, all over the city. . . .

A siren cut through the air, and Screech swooped down.

Police car! he said.

"Run!" hissed Caw, grabbing Lydia's arm.

Blue light spun around the corner ahead, so they doubled back, down a cobbled street where vents on the side of a building blasted hot air into the night. Caw flattened himself against the wall and peered through the billowing water vapor. The sirens died, but the lights were still flashing. Slowly, the police car turned into their street.

"No, no," muttered Caw. They sprinted away from their hiding place, and the car's engine roared after them.

"This way!" said Caw, skidding around a corner and climbing a set of steps. He grabbed Lydia's hand and tugged her after him. They ran across a small ornamental garden as the police car screeched to a halt. They jumped over some flower beds, then crossed another road, running under an arch and along an enclosed row of shops. Trash littered the ground, kicked up by a gusting breeze. Caw heard footsteps coming after them and saw a flashlight jolting in the darkness.

"D'you see which way they went?" shouted a voice.

"No," called another. "You check that way."

Caw and Lydia came out of the far end of the shops. Caw was breathing hard and Lydia was bent double, hands on her knees.

Across the street was a nightclub, a neon sign glowing above the door.

"I think we lost them," said Caw as Lydia straightened up, "but we should keep moving."

"Okay," said Lydia, pushing a lock of hair off her sticky forehead.

They set off again. Caw was still looking back as they rounded a corner and walked straight into a couple holding hands. He stumbled and caught himself against Lydia.

"Excuse me," he muttered.

"Hey there!" said the woman.

She was wearing high heels and some sort of fur coat, and her lips were bright red. The man she was with was in a black suit, his cheeks flushed. Caw guessed he was drunk. "Keep walking," he said to Lydia.

They hurried away. "Honey," Caw heard the woman say, "isn't that the missing girl from the news?"

Caw broke into a jog, taking Lydia by the arm. The low-rise bars and clubs and vacant shop fronts gave way to the business district. It was completely deserted, the skyscrapers standing like sentinels guarding each side of the street. Their black windows reflected a hundred Caws back at him. His ears were pricked for any more sirens, but no sounds disturbed the night.

"Can we slow down now?" Lydia gasped. "We need to be careful. Our faces . . . they're too well known."

Caw nodded grimly.

Beyond the steel-and-glass office buildings, the city rose into several forested slopes dotted with residential houses.

"We're looking for Quaker, right? Herrick Hill is this way," said Lydia, pointing up a road lined with trees. "Hey, what's the matter?"

Caw had paused at the roadside. "Nothing," he said. "It's just . . . I've never been farther than this before."

Lydia gave him a smile, then crossed the road. Caw followed her.

It was strangely quiet now that they'd left the bustle of the city center. Even the air smelled different—cleaner, fresher. There were no streetlights, and soon there were no sidewalks either, as Caw and Lydia followed the edge of the road winding up the hill. The crows were almost invisible as they flew between the branches of the pines. Caw stared into the trees, but he couldn't see farther than a few yards before the darkness swallowed the trunks. Occasionally they passed a driveway with the dim shape of a house set well back from the road.

Caw's nerves tingled, and he threw frequent glances over his shoulder. Going anywhere new made him anxious, and the more distance they put between themselves and Blackstone Park, the more he worried.

"You're sure this is the way?" he asked. His voice sounded thin and hollow.

Lydia nodded. "You can't miss Gort House," she said. "It's one of the oldest in the city. My dad and I sometimes come this way on the weekends—we take Benjy for long walks out in the country." Her face froze. "I mean, we *took* Benjy for walks."

Caw glanced at her, expecting to see her fighting back tears. Instead, she just looked more determined.

Lydia was right—Gort House was unmistakable. The first they saw of it was a tall wall lined with razor wire, with a double-spiked gate. The place looked like it had once been as impenetrable as a fortress—maybe this was what had kept Quaker safe from the Spinning Man's followers during Dark Summer. But it appeared the cat feral had let the place go since then. Some of the spikes on the gate had broken off, leaving harmless stumps behind.

As they got closer, they saw a long drive beyond the gate, offering a view up to the house. It stood on the top of the hill, silhouetted against the skyline. There was a moss-covered fountain in the middle of the front courtyard, and the babbling water glistened like silver in the moonlight. The house was three stories tall, with a tower at each corner and battlements running across the top. Once it might have been painted bright blue, but time had faded and chipped that away until all that remained was a dull gray. Arched windows sat at irregular heights across the front and sides, and ivy crept over the walls like it was trying to smother them. A single window on the second floor was dimly illuminated.

"Shall we?" said Lydia, placing a hand on one of the railings.

Caw nodded. He boosted Lydia to the top, then scrambled up after her.

"You're stronger than you look," said Lydia, carefully climbing over the section of the gate where the spikes had fallen away.

Caw blushed as Lydia lowered herself over the other side. He followed, dropping and landing in a silent crouch.

Not all the grounds of Gort House had been left to molder. Sculpted gardens lined the driveway up to the front of the house, the hedges all elaborately shaped into cats. Caw noticed that the fountain was a sculpture of cats playing, the water spouting from their mouths. His footsteps crunched on the gravel path. He couldn't help feeling like they were being watched from one of the many windows. His pulse raced as he lifted the heavy knocker, a paw shaped in cold iron.

Thunk! Thunk! The sound of the metal was deafening.

Caw took a step back and waited. His crows were perched high on one of the turrets, out of sight. *Weird,* he thought. *Yesterday they'd have been dead set against a trip like this. But they're barely saying a word.*

It was almost as if, now that the truth was out, they were willing to go along with his wishes. Whether that was because their respect for him had grown, he couldn't tell. Perhaps it was just that he was being more stubborn.

The sound of footsteps came from within, then the squeal of a key turning. The door opened with a creak, just a few inches, and a green-eyed cat slunk out, winding itself around Caw's legs.

Caw's gaze traveled up a pair of baggy purple trousers to a substantial gut hemmed in by a matching purple waistcoat with quartz buttons. Over the top, the man wore a woolen jacket the color of a tangerine. His face was broad and ruddy cheeked, with a bushy salt-and-pepper mustache twisted at the ends to look like whiskers. His small eyes glinted suspiciously, one slightly magnified by a silver-chained monocle.

The cat at Caw's ankle slipped back inside. A moment later it hopped up and rested on the man's shoulder.

"Felix Quaker?" said Caw.

"And who might you be?"

Caw hesitated, wishing he'd thought this through more. Everything depended on what he said next.

"What, cat got your tongue?" snapped the man. He smiled creepily, and Caw caught a glimpse of small, spiky teeth behind his lips.

"My name is Caw," he said. "I'm a feral just like you, and—"

The door slammed shut.

Lydia banged the knocker again. "We need to talk to you," she called through the door.

"That's too bad, my dear," said the man from inside. "Because I don't want anything to do with *you!*"

"Please!" said Caw. "We know you're a feral."

"I don't know what you're blathering about. I'm calling the police. You'd best get away from here before they arrive."

Caw shot a glance at Lydia. "He won't call them," she whispered. "Let's find another way in."

They trod as quietly as possible around the side of the house. Halfway around, Glum squawked from a narrow ledge above.

Window on the second floor. It's not closed properly.

"Perfect!" Caw whispered.

Luckily, the ivy was thick enough to get a firm grip, and placing his hands carefully among the tangle of branches, Caw managed to pick his way up. Lydia followed, looking uncertain. "Don't worry," he told her. "It'll hold your weight." He'd climbed much weaker patches of ivy back in the park.

He found the window slightly ajar. The frame was made of lead, and the glass was so old it had distorted out of shape. Caw prized it open. He couldn't make out much in the room beyond, apart from what looked like glass cases on tables.

Caw hopped onto the ledge and reached down to pull Lydia up. She wobbled slightly, but he kept a firm grip on her arm and then she climbed through the window first. The three crows landed beside Caw in a gust of beating black and white wings. They jostled on the window ledge.

"You'd better stay outside," said Caw.

If we must, said Glum, settling onto his belly feathers. *But be careful.*

"I will," he said.

Screech shuffled alongside him. *Move over, chubby.*

"Hey, check this out!" whispered Lydia.

Caw climbed into the room and saw her standing beside one of the glass cases. There was nothing else in the room but the tables and the cases. Caw followed Lydia's pointing finger and gasped. Inside the case, lit by moonlight, was a small, wizened hand. "You think it's real?" he said.

Lydia shrugged, moving to the next case, which contained a curved shield made of glass or crystal, maybe even diamond, with hairs embedded inside. Caw had never seen anything like it. The third case held a mask, made of a thin sheet of metal and shaped into the face of a lion.

"I think that's gold," said Lydia. "What on earth is this place?"

"Crumb said Quaker collects stuff on ferals," said Caw. "But this doesn't look like just some old junk. These things seem valuable. I wonder what else he's hiding here?"

He went to the door and eased the handle down. It opened smoothly onto a carpeted hallway above a set of sweeping stairs, with a banister ornately carved from dark wood. Huge portraits lined the walls, men and women in different historical dress. Were they all ferals? There were black statues of cats, positioned on plinths where the stairs turned. One suddenly moved, and Caw realized it was alive. It descended the steps like a shadow.

The carpet cushioned Caw's footsteps as he crept out of the room. He turned across a landing toward another set of stairs, leading up. More glass cases lined the walls of the landing, and several doors led off it, all closed. Caw was sure he'd never been here before, yet there was something weirdly familiar about the house. He put his foot on the first step leading upward.

Somewhere below a piano tinkled discordantly, then paused.

"Where are you going?" whispered Lydia. "Sounds like Quaker's downstairs."

Caw rested a hand on the banister. His feet moved on, drawing him toward the top of the house—but he didn't know why.

"Hey," hissed Lydia. "Don't you want to look at these?" She was standing by one of the cases, nose pressed to the side. "This one's a spider necklace!"

A wordless summons seemed to beckon Caw, calling him toward the top of the stairs. "I just thought—y'know—spiders and all," said Lydia behind him, her voice dim and distant.

Caw climbed the steps. At the top there was nothing—just a small square landing of bare floorboards and no windows.

"Caw, come back!" called Lydia in an urgent whisper. "Why are you acting so weird?"

He walked to the wall and ran his hands over its uneven surface. He expected it to be cold, but it wasn't. Lydia hurried up the stairs behind him.

"Caw?" she said. "Can you even hear me?"

He let his palm rest on the wall.

"You're scaring me," said Lydia. "What's going on?"

Caw pressed hard, and a section of the wall gave way—a narrow hidden door that swung inward on noiseless hinges. The blood pumping through Caw's temples subsided.

"How did you know that was there?" said Lydia.

"I didn't," said Caw, stepping through. Or perhaps, somehow, he did.

The room was gloomy, without any sort of light. It had to be in one of the towers, because it was perfectly round, with a single window high up on the wall. It was more like a cell than anything. There was a rickety chair and an old wardrobe, plus a stained sink. But all these details seemed to fade away when Caw's eyes rested on the object in the center of the room.

It was a glass case containing a red velvet cushion. And on top of the cushion lay a sword almost a yard long, its blade black and slightly curved—wide at its base, sharpening to a deadly point. It looked like some ancient artifact dug up from the earth and polished until its surfaces gleamed. The hilt was protected by several looping metal talons and covered in a thin layer of what looked like black leather. There was writing engraved along the length of the blade.

"What does it say?" he asked. His voice was little more than a croak.

Lydia peered closer. "It's some strange language," she said. "Weird symbols. Listen, there's a huge double-headed ax downstairs. Come and see!"

But Caw wasn't interested in any ax. He didn't know how, but he *knew* this sword was important. And somehow he knew exactly the feel of it, the weight, without even holding it. He knew that the sword had been calling him to this room. It *wanted* to be found. He reached out toward the case.

"Are you sure you should be doing this?" asked Lydia.

"Yes," said Caw. As his fingers touched the glass, blinding light filled his head, making him stagger back. Images from his dream flashed behind his eyes—his mother's mouth stretched in fear; his father's fingers clawing at his throat; the spider ring on the long finger of the Spinning Man.

"Caw! Someone's coming!" Lydia gasped.

Caw blinked the visions away. Footsteps. Then there were cats streaming into the room, hissing and wailing. The narrow door burst open wide and Felix Quaker surged through. "I can explain—" Caw began.

Quaker grabbed him by the ear. "How dare you break in here!" he said. "Get out!"

He hauled Caw toward the door. Pain burned at the side of Caw's head. He was dimly aware of Lydia following. "Don't hurt him, please!" she was saying. "We only want to talk."

Quaker dragged Caw out of the room and into the hallway. Caw stumbled to keep his balance, bent over almost double to stop his ear from being torn off his head. The cats flooded after them, yowling all the time.

"You little rats!" Quaker snarled. "I've a good mind to— What on earth?"

Caw heard the whip crack of wings, and Quaker stumbled back, as Milky, Glum, and Screech shot into the room. "No! Don't!" Caw said as the crows descended on the cat feral. At the same time several cats leaped into the air. Caw flinched as they dragged the flailing crows to the ground, pinning them easily. Quaker straightened his waistcoat, licking his lips as he surveyed the crows.

"Please!" Caw said. "The crows are just trying to help me!"

The cats looked up to their master, eyes gleaming hungrily.

"Maybe it's time to give my darlings a treat," said Quaker, his voice cold. "After all, this is my house."

Do your worst, cat talker, said Glum, squirming under a paw.

Caw, said Milky calmly. *Leave us. Go now.*

The white crow's voice took Caw by surprise. It gave him courage. He hadn't come all this way just to desert his crows. "I'm not going anywhere," he said. "I came here to talk to Felix Quaker about my parents and the Spinning Man."

Caw, you must flee this place! said Milky, his voice more urgent.

Quaker twisted the ends of his mustache and looked at Caw curiously. "I admire your tenacity, my boy, but as I told you—I have nothing to say. Now get out of my—"

The front door below crashed open with a bang. Between the wide columns of the balustrade, Caw saw three drooling attack dogs stalking through the entrance hall. A shadow fell on the carpet from outside, and then Jawbone's huge bulk stepped over the threshold.

13

Caw jerked back out of sight. "It's Jawbone!" he said in a whisper.

Quaker's whole demeanor changed at once. He seemed to transform from an eccentric hermit to a creature of stealth, moving like liquid to press himself against a wall. He shot a glance down the stairway and made a clicking sound in his throat. Instantly, his cats sprang up to gather at his side, releasing the crows. Glum let out a pained squawk, and the dogs below growled.

"Looks like you've grown lazy in your old age, Quaker," said Jawbone. "You don't want to let guys like me get into your hideout. Now come out, little kitty. I know you're here. My pretties can smell you."

Felix Quaker pulled Caw's ear up to his lips. "You've done enough damage. Now get out while you still can!"

"But—" Caw began.

The sound of the snarling dogs grew closer.

"Come on!" said Lydia. She darted downstairs into the room with the glass cases, and Caw followed with his crows.

"Don't bother running from us, Quaker!" bellowed Jawbone.

"You'll only make them angry!"

At the door of the room, Caw stopped. Lydia was already on the window ledge. But something made him drag his feet. The blade—it was calling to him. He had to have it. "Go on without me!" he yelled to Lydia, turning back.

"Wait!" she called. "Where are . . ."

Her voice died as Caw dashed past Quaker and his cats and up the stairs. He bounded into the turret room. *Caw, leave it!* cried Glum, flapping around the room.

Caw frantically examined the locked case. Nothing to break it with . . . Quaker must have the key. . . .

From below, he heard the screeching of the cats as they attacked, muffled by growling and snapping dogs. "You'll pay if you hurt a single one of them!" shouted Quaker.

The growling stopped suddenly.

"Now, time for a little chat," said Jawbone. "You thought you had us fooled, didn't you? Acting like some doddery old madman. But we know what you've got locked away. Scuttle's roaches crawled into this dump and found it." His voice went dangerously quiet. "So no more games now. Take me to the Crow's Beak."

Caw heard a couple of heavy thumps. Quaker howled. "Get out of my house, you mangy brute," he spat, his voice twisted with pain.

Caw's eyes fell on the sword. *The Crow's Beak.* This weapon— this was what Quaker was hiding. The words spoke to something

157

deep within him. It was his, this blade. The crow talker's sword.

"Quit stalling, Quaker," said Jawbone. "Or shall I call Scuttle in? His friends will burrow through your ears and eat your brain. You'll be able to *feel* them long after you can even scream. Or Mamba? One bite from her snakes and you'll be paralyzed. I swear to you, Quaker, if I have to skin every cat in this house, one by one, I'll do it. Whatever it takes to make you talk."

There was a pause.

"Up there," the cat feral replied, his voice suddenly flat.

Caw's skin went cold. There was nowhere to run. He climbed onto the chair, then reached for the window. Too high. Even if he jumped, he wouldn't be able to reach it.

Screech flapped onto the wardrobe. He didn't need to speak—Caw understood. He hurried across the room as Jawbone's footsteps thumped up the stairs. Caw threw open the door and leaped inside. The crows slipped in as well, and Caw quickly pulled the door shut. He brought his eye to the crack.

Jawbone shoved Quaker into the room, and the man's monocle fell loose and landed on the floor with a brittle *ping*. The dogs stopped at the door, sniffing the air. The cat feral was bleeding from both nostrils, and an angry welt had risen under his eye.

Caw swallowed thickly as he saw that one of the dogs had blood around its sagging black lips. Clearly one of Quaker's cats had been unlucky.

If they smell me, it's over, thought Caw.

But the dogs seemed cautious—almost fearful. Their tails hung between their legs, and they didn't cross the threshold. All three were staring at the Crow's Beak.

Jawbone walked around the room, the timber floorboards creaking with every step. He circled the glass case. "Where's the key?" he snapped, holding out a shovel-like hand.

"It's downstairs in my study," said Quaker, wiping blood from his nose with a handkerchief. "If you want it, you can fetch it yourself."

Behind the cat feral, the three dogs growled.

Jawbone grinned, his tattooed face transforming into a hideous mask. He folded his open palm into a fist and lifted it high above Quaker's head like a wrecking ball. Caw could barely watch. Was the convict going to crush the old man's skull right in front of him?

Then Jawbone turned on his heel and brought his hand down onto the glass case. It splintered with a crash, throwing shards across the room. "Looks like I don't need it," he said.

As Jawbone reached in and seized the hilt of the Crow's Beak, Caw felt a stab of anger mixed with something else—envy. He had to stop himself from leaping out and attacking the dog feral on the spot.

Jawbone turned the blade in the meager light from the bulb above, examining it closely. A shimmer passed along the metal, illuminating the strange letters. "Doesn't look like much to me," he said. "A child's toy."

"It's priceless," hissed Felix Quaker. "In the wrong hands—"

"Spare me," said Jawbone. "I know what it is." He shoved the sword down through his belt. Caw gritted his teeth.

"You have what you came for," said Quaker, his voice heavy with exhaustion. "Now leave."

Jawbone nodded thoughtfully, but then his head jerked down. He stooped toward the floor. "What's this?" he said.

As he stood again, Quaker's eyes shot for a split second toward the wardrobe. Jawbone was holding a black feather.

A scream of fear lodged in Caw's throat.

"The crow talker is here," said Jawbone. It wasn't a question, but a statement of fact.

Quaker shook his head.

"You're a bad liar," said Jawbone. "My colleagues will find her soon enough."

Quaker frowned, and Caw realized the cat feral was confused as well.

Her?

"You won't find her!" said Quaker suddenly. Jawbone shoved him out of his way and strode toward the door. Then he paused and spoke without turning around.

"They say you cat ferals have nine lives. Let's see, shall we?"

"What?" said Quaker, darting back. There was a crunch as he trod on his own monocle.

Jawbone laid a hand on each of the dogs' heads in turn. As he did so, their ears went back and they lifted their tails. "Finish him off," he said, and left the room.

"No!" Quaker cried.

The dogs entered, fanning out. Caw saw Felix Quaker snatch up the chair and brandish it in front of him. It only made the dogs growl with more menace.

"Orion!" said Quaker, swishing the chair back and forth. "Vespa! Monty! Claws out!"

One of the dogs leaped up toward his face, and Quaker sidestepped it deftly. An instant later, a second dog's teeth fastened over his sleeve and tore a section away.

Caw pushed open the wardrobe doors, letting out a yell to distract the dogs. At the same time, he willed his crows to attack. They flew out, raking their talons at the dogs' eyes and stabbing with their beaks. Caw grabbed Quaker and pulled him out of the room. The crows swooped after them, and the moment they were through, Quaker slammed the door closed.

On the other side they heard the dogs snarling and throwing themselves against the wood, shaking the door in its frame. Three cats finally darted up the stairs, hissing, but they stopped as Quaker wearily waved a hand.

"Some use you three were!" he said.

The cats responded with a series of indignant purrs.

"Well, you would say that," said Quaker. "Lucky for me, the crows were here." He turned to Caw. "What I can't understand is why Jawbone called the crow talker *her*. . . . I was only too happy to assist in misleading him, but—"

"Lydia!" interrupted Caw. "They must think Lydia is the crow feral! We need to find her."

"Now hold on," said Quaker, but Caw was already starting down the stairs.

Lydia's shouts cut through the house, making Caw's heart jolt. He took the stairs two at a time, leaving his crows behind and vaulting over the turn in the banister, light as air. It felt as though a wind was carrying him along, giving him a speed he wasn't used to.

On the landing, he saw a cat lying dead in a pool of blood.

Wait! called Glum.

Caw took the next flight to the first floor in two bounds and hit the ground running. He sped through the front door, which hung askew on its hinges. Screech shot ahead of him, flapping hard.

At the bottom of the driveway, Jawbone was striding toward a van. Mamba sat in the front seat, while Scuttle bundled Lydia in through a sliding side door. She kicked madly, screaming, "Let me go! Get your hands off me!"

Jawbone slid the door closed behind them.

Caw ran as fast as he could, but Jawbone was already climbing into the front seat. They hadn't even seen him.

"Stop!" Caw yelled.

But the van's tires spun, kicking up gravel and smoke. Then the van sped through the busted-open gates and away down the hill. Caw sprinted after them, his hopes vanishing as the vehicle's rear lights faded into the distance. With his chest on fire, he stumbled to a halt in the middle of the road.

"No . . . please . . . ," he said.

Not Lydia too.

Milky fluttered out of the sky and landed on his arm, and then Glum and Screech descended too.

"They think she's the crow talker," said Caw.

And they'll discover soon enough that she isn't, said Glum.

Caw picked himself up. "What will they do then?"

Glum didn't speak for a long time.

We should go back to the house, he said finally. *The cat talker must be able to help.*

Caw nodded, but he noticed that Glum hadn't answered his question.

Caw found Felix Quaker in the hallway, carrying the dead cat in his arms. He glanced up as Caw approached.

"They took her," Caw said in a hollow voice. "Please . . . she's the only friend I've got. Help me get her back."

Quaker regarded Caw for a moment and then looked back at the cat in his arms. He stroked her bloodied fur gently. "She was called Helena," he said. "It's been fifteen years since I found her as a stray."

"I'm sorry," said Caw. "I know what it's like to lose someone."

"Yes . . . I suppose you must," said Quaker.

"Please don't make me go through it again," Caw pleaded. "Lydia is still alive. We can still save her."

Quaker's eyes fell on the crows, perched on the banister. "She'll keep, for now. First, we need to talk. Come with me, crow talker."

Caw clenched his fists as the cat feral walked from the room. He wanted to run out into the street, to start tracking the prisoners down straightaway. But he knew that Quaker might be the only one who'd know how to find them. So—against all his instincts—Caw followed.

The dogs' barks still rang through the house as Felix Quaker led Caw to a cellar kitchen with a cobbled floor and a simple wooden table. The crows flew in and landed on the edge of the sink. Quaker placed the dead cat softly on a sheet of newspaper in front of a huge hearth. A dozen other cats emerged and gathered around the corpse of their friend, mewing softly. The cat feral was unrecognizable from the immaculately dressed man who had answered the door less than an hour before. His wrist was bleeding from the dog bite, blood crusted under his nose, and his crisply ironed clothes were wrinkled and torn.

He turned his narrowed eyes on Caw. "So tell me, why do they think your friend is the crow feral?"

"I suppose . . . every time they saw me with the crows, she was there too," said Caw, realizing it was true as he said it. "In fact, that first time in the alleyway, they didn't see me at all—just Lydia. When Jawbone attacked her dad, they must have thought it was her calling the crows to protect him.

"And then at the Strickhams' house, Mamba must have seen my crows waiting outside . . . but she didn't see me *then* either. So of course she thought they were Lydia's."

He wanted to scream at the unfairness of it all. If only he had sent her back to Crumb's hideout, none of this would have happened.

"I see," said Quaker. "And how did you find me?"

"Miss Wallace," Caw said quietly. "Before . . ."

"The incident at the library," said Quaker. He ran a cloth under the tap and dabbed his bloody nose. "I read about it. The police didn't give any details, though. You knew her too?"

Caw nodded. "Jawbone and his friends killed her," he said.

"Savages!" said Quaker, flashing his sharp teeth in a grimace. "The librarian was a capable woman. I use the library often for my research. Of course, she never knew who *I* really was." He tossed the cloth in the sink. "Two days ago, I was taking out some books when I saw a drawing on her desk."

"A spider?" said Caw.

Quaker looked up sharply. "Yes! How do you—"

"We drew it," said Caw. "Me and Lydia."

Quaker's eyebrows rose a fraction. "Well, I must have given quite a start when I saw it, because the librarian asked what it meant to me. I didn't want anything to do with it, of course. I told her as much, quite firmly. Then I left in a hurry."

"She must have guessed that you knew something about it. She wrote your name underneath that drawing," said Caw. "She was holding it when they killed her."

Quaker looked away as though unable to meet Caw's eyes. The dogs' barking had become less frequent, and Quaker glanced upward. "They'll calm down eventually," he said. "I never liked dogs, but they're mostly harmless away from their feral's influence."

Caw had so many questions, he hardly knew where to start. And how were any of them going to help Lydia?

"So you know Jawbone?" he said.

"I've run into the likes of him in the past," said Quaker. "That strand of dog talker has always been nasty."

"There are others?" said Caw.

Felix Quaker sat heavily on a chair. "You'll find a kettle on the range with hot water, and tea leaves in that jar on the shelf." He pointed. "I can't talk about ferals without a decent cup of tea in my hand."

Begrudgingly, Caw fetched the jar and found two cups. He

began to empty some of the dried leaves into them.

"Hold on there!" said Quaker. "You've not done this before, I see. Watch and learn!"

Caw stepped back and let the cat feral take over. He scooped the leaves into a metal object with holes in the side, then put that into a small pot and filled it with steaming water.

"I suppose I owe you my thanks," said Quaker. "Jawbone's dogs would have killed me if it weren't for your crows."

"Well, I'd be dead too, if you'd told him I was in that wardrobe," said Caw.

Quaker leaned closer to Caw, sniffed deeply, then nodded. "I didn't recognize you at first, but I should have. The resemblance is uncanny."

Caw's neck prickled. "You knew my parents?"

Quaker poured the amber liquid into two cups and pushed one across the table to Caw. "I did indeed, Jack."

"Jack?" said Caw, sitting up straighter.

"I suppose you don't use that name anymore," said Quaker. He sipped his tea and purred contentedly. "I remember you as a baby. Jack Carmichael, son of Elizabeth and Richard. They were clever people. Brave, too—perhaps a bit too much so, at the end."

Caw swallowed and fought back the threat of tears. He turned his attention to the cup of tea. Taking a sip, he let the strange flavor settle on his tongue and winced.

"Not a fan, I see?" said Quaker, smiling. "Neither was your mother."

Caw sat up straighter.

"Well, we shan't waste it," said Quaker, snatching the cup toward his own. He took another sip of tea. "You know, I thought the crow line had ended. After the events of the Dark Summer, I went to your house. You were all gone, but the signs were there. The webs, so thick I had to use an ax to get through the door." Quaker shook his head at the memory. "What a waste of talent. If only your mother had kept herself barricaded inside, as I did, maybe she'd still be alive, but—"

Quaker stopped midsentence and seemed to notice the stricken look on Caw's face. When he spoke again, his voice was softer. "As I said, they were brave." He took another sip of tea. But for an instant, Caw thought he almost looked ashamed.

"Why did you go to my parents' house?" asked Caw.

"To recover the Crow's Beak, of course," said Quaker.

"That sword."

The cat feral nodded. "Luckily for me, your mother had hidden it well."

"What is it?" asked Caw. "A weapon?"

Quaker's eyes widened a little, then narrowed again. "It's tragic that you know so little about your heritage, Jack."

Caw felt a blush rise to his cheeks. "Then *tell* me."

"The Crow's Beak might look like a weapon, but in fact it's more of a tool—a key—passed down between crow ferals since ancient times, when Blackstone was just fields and a river. It can cut through the veil that separates this world and the other."

"The *other*?" said Caw.

Milky gave a low squawk from the edge of the sink, and the two crows on either side glanced at him nervously.

Quaker's cup rattled on its saucer as he placed it down. He stared hard at Caw, and the cats by the hearth turned their eyes to their master, their ears pricked up and alert. "The Land of the Dead," he said.

Caw felt his stomach twist.

The cat feral continued, glancing briefly at Milky. "Crows have always been special," he said. "They are the only creatures that can cross back and forth between the lands."

"But what is the Land of the Dead?" asked Caw.

"What does it sound like?"

The hairs on Caw's neck rose. "The afterlife?"

"You can call it that if you like."

"That doesn't make sense."

"You don't believe me?" said Quaker. "Your white friend there knows I'm telling the truth."

Milky stared at them.

"He doesn't talk much, I see," said Quaker. "Well, his feathers do the talking for him. He's white like that because he's one of the few to have visited the Land of the Dead and come back."

Caw looked at Milky with new eyes. Could it be true?

"Say I believe you," he said carefully. "What's this place like?"

"Better ask him," said Quaker, pointing at Milky.

Milky took off and landed on the table between them, talons clicking on the wood.

"Look into his eyes," said Quaker. "Look hard."

Milky cocked his head. Caw felt strange with Quaker and the animals watching, but all the same he stared into the crow's pale left eye. "What have you got to show me, Milky?" he said softly.

At first he saw nothing. Then, in the depths of the pale orb, shapes began to swirl. He stared harder, and the rest of the room faded as the eye seemed to suck him in. Caw felt like he was floating, then falling, falling, into the depths of a misty sky. He saw shapes through the fog—woodland, branches, the ground covered in layers of black leaves.

"Do you see it?" said Quaker's voice, from somewhere in the distance.

Caw nodded, unable to break away from Milky's gaze. Through the mists he saw faces among the trees, figures drifting between the trunks. Two turned toward him, and he floated closer. They reached their arms out and murmured his name softly. "Jack?"

It was his mother. He glimpsed her face through the mist—her large, dark eyes, her kind smile. Then his father as well, his serious, clean-shaven features, with a slight dimple in his chin. The rest of their bodies were indistinct, but their faces called to him. "Jack, come to us," they said together.

Just as he was about to fall into their embrace, another face appeared behind them. Caw's heart lurched in horror, for there stood the Spinning Man, his spider hands sinking into Caw's parents' shoulders, yanking them away. His eyes were black and glittering, and his gaze was fixed on Caw.

Caw jolted backward with a gasp and almost fell off his chair. He was in the kitchen again, and Milky was watching him, head still cocked.

"The Spinning Man," said Caw. "I saw him!"

"He is waiting for you," said Quaker gravely.

"Me? Why?"

"Why do you think?" said Quaker. "Only the crow talker can wield the Crow's Beak."

"And bring him back," said Caw in a rush of understanding. "If I cut through the veil, he can return. That's why his followers need the crow talker."

Felix Quaker nodded and took a last gulp of tea, setting the cup down with finality. "Their mistake with the girl has bought you a little time, but they will come back for you soon enough."

"That may be true," Caw said, standing. "But I'm not planning on hiding away like you. Thanks for the tea, but I need to go now. I need to find Lydia."

Quaker reached down to stroke a ginger tomcat who was winding around his ankles. "My place is here," he said. "I've helped you all I can."

A light knock at the doorway made them both look up. Crumb was waiting at the threshold of the kitchen, Pip standing beside him.

"Yet more intruders, I see," said Quaker.

"The front door was wide open," said Crumb. "Looks like you've had some unwelcome visitors. Although I guess all visitors are unwelcome here." His glance passed over Caw and the crows, and his expression hardened. "Where's Lydia?"

"They took her," said Caw grimly. "They think she's the crow feral."

Crumb's face betrayed little emotion, other than a slight flaring of his nostrils, but Pip pushed past him, pointing angrily at Caw.

"You should have stayed with us, stupid," he said. "We said you weren't ready!"

"And you were right," said Caw, cowed by the little boy's stinging words. "But I'm going to make up for it."

"And how will you do that?" said Pip.

"You have to teach me everything you can," Caw said to Crumb. "Fast. Please, you have to help me. *Somebody* has to help me." He glanced over at Quaker, but the cat feral wouldn't meet his gaze.

"Please, Crumb," Caw repeated. "Lydia's life depends on it."

Crumb seemed to be deep in thought, his eyes fixed on the ground. Caw held his breath. Finally the pigeon feral met his gaze again. "Very well, crow talker," he said. "But I warn you—it's going to hurt."

14

In the hour after dawn, Blackstone stirred to life like a creature shaking off slumber. Buses rumbled through the streets, carrying huddled passengers home from their night shifts or off to early starts. Litter blew through the alleys, and the homeless cowered in flimsy cardboard shelters, beneath the bridges and in doorways, snatching their last few hours of undisturbed sleep. Shopkeepers pulled up shutters with loud bangs.

Caw ached from head to foot as they descended Herrick Hill and entered the financial district, no longer last night's ghost town of steel and glass, but thronging with men and women in suits, streaming like insects into the giant anthills of their offices. They all seemed far too busy to even notice the strange trio—the scruffy man and the two boys—walking in their midst or the odd collection of birds circling overhead.

Caw's bones seemed loose and rattling, and the tendons between his muscles screamed with every step. He had scratches over every bit of exposed skin. But he could hardly complain. He had asked Crumb to teach him, and the lessons had been just as painful as promised. They'd practiced in Felix Quaker's huge back garden—the cat feral had at least agreed to help in that small way. So for several hours it had been Caw against Crumb, crow versus pigeon, the ferals and their creatures doing battle under the stars.

Some things had come quickly—he could summon hundreds of crows with just a thought now—but Crumb was always one step ahead. It was like a dance to which Caw didn't know the steps, and he was so busy listening for the rhythm that his feet tripped over each other. The pigeon talker had been merciless in his assaults, swatting the crows aside, sending his birds to rake Caw with claws and beaks. At one point the pigeons had even lifted Caw from the ground and hurled him into a bush. He had a palm-sized bruise under his ribs to remind him of that.

Quaker and Pip had watched from the sidelines with a mixture of wry amusement and the occasional sympathetic grimace. The sight of their mice and cats sitting beside one another had looked distinctly odd, but both ferals kept their creatures in check. Caw knew what Quaker was thinking—that Caw was useless, a pale shadow of his mother and her abilities.

The cat feral had slowly, very slowly warmed up to their invasion of his privacy and eventually was regaling them with stories of Black Corvus, the greatest crow talker of all. Apparently he had been so powerful that he could control several murders of crows at once, and even, according to some sources, become a crow himself.

Crumb had said that was nonsense, and he and Quaker had argued about what was a legend and what was historical fact for a good ten minutes. At least it had given Caw a break from the fighting.

"Chin up," said the pigeon talker as they reached a deserted road running between old wharves by the river.

"It hurts to keep my chin up," grumbled Caw. "You dropped me on my head, remember?"

Pip giggled. "That *was* a bit mean."

"You definitely improved," said Crumb. "By the time we finished, you weren't crying out half as loudly as at the start." He pointed up at a brick bridge spanning the street. "We're here."

"What's here?" said Caw.

Crumb shared a look with Pip. "You'll see soon enough."

He summoned a couple of pigeons to his arm. "Watch the ends of the street. Any police, you raise the alarm."

The pigeons cooed in reply and flew in opposite directions.

"Follow me," said Crumb.

They climbed a set of steps into an abandoned monorail station, half enclosed by a fixed metal awning covering the tracks. Old railcars squatted in a siding, rusted and covered in graffiti, their windows smashed. Caw's three crows settled on the top of a dented ticket booth. Though the risen sun was invisible behind buildings, its morning light suffused the air with a delicate, almost opalescent light.

I could do with a rest! said Screech. *I swear my feathers ache.*

Mine too, said Glum. *Those pigeons are tougher than they look.*

"Right," said Crumb. "Let's see what you've learned."

"Again?" said Caw.

Crumb walked to the far end of the track. "Focus, crow talker," he said seriously.

Pip had placed himself out of the way on the edge of the tracks overlooking the street, a mouse perched on each shoulder. "At least make a fight of it," he called. "I'm bored with watching you get hurt."

Caw glared at him, and the mouse talker gave him a wink.

I'll show them, thought Caw. He closed his eyes and sent out his summons. Within seconds the air filled with crows. They alighted across his arms and on the ground around him. With a hand signal, he separated them into two lines—one to attack, the other to stay beside him and defend—just as Crumb had taught him.

"Good!" said Crumb. Then, without warning, he opened a hand and his pigeons descended in a wave.

Caw threw his first volley of crows to meet them. They clashed midair in a blurred mass of gray and black feathers, screeching and squawking madly. Hidden from view, Caw ran sideways, taking shelter behind a leaning kiosk. He sent his remaining crows in a roundabout swarm, hoping to attack Crumb from the side. But Crumb was ready. A wall of his pigeons lifted from the ground, talons outstretched. The older feral rolled beneath the melee and stood on the other side. "Not bad, Caw!" he said. "Caw?"

Caw grinned with satisfaction as he peered out. Crumb hadn't seen him.

A soft warble made him look up. A pigeon perched on top of the kiosk, staring down at him.

"Ah, there you are," said Crumb. "Thanks, Bobbin."

Quickly, Caw summoned more crows. A few detached from their battles with the pigeons. But at the same time he saw an army of new pigeons descending from a rooftop nearby.

They swooped low, right toward him.

He thinks he's got me, but he's wrong.

Caw lifted his right hand, and the reserves he had under the bridge rose in a black cloud. He left them to intercept the pigeon wave. At the same time, he marshaled Screech, Glum, and Milky to come from behind Crumb. He saw them land on the pigeon talker's back, flapping their wings in his face and knocking him off balance. *Yes!* He punched the air.

Crumb cried out in shock as his knees hit the platform, and his pigeon flocks scattered into disarray. A dozen swept past Caw's head, flying low. Caw ducked and then saw it—the pigeons were heading straight for Pip. The small boy swiveled and cried out as the birds surged past him, flipping him around and making him stagger. Caw felt a spike of panic as he saw one leg slip from the trackside. Pip's arms flailed for balance, and then he toppled over the edge, letting out a thin scream.

"Pip!" bellowed Crumb.

"Help him!" Caw yelled, thrusting out an arm for any crow that was listening. They spilled over the railway track like a wave of midnight. He held his breath, waiting for a thud.

A second passed. Then another.

On the third, the crows rose with Pip squirming in their talons. They set him down carefully on the platform. The boy's face was white as he straightened his clothes.

Crumb rushed to the mouse feral, pigeons fluttering away on all sides. He grabbed Pip and pulled him close, then shot a glance at Caw and nodded, his eyes full of relief. "I think the duel's over," he said. "You've proved yourself, crow talker."

Go, Caw! called Screech.

You done good, said Glum.

Caw flushed with pride, his heart thumping from the fight. Pip detached himself from Crumb. "I thought I was dead for sure," he said, blowing out his cheeks. "Thank you, Caw."

Caw smiled. "Thank the crows," he said.

"No, it was you," said Pip. He dropped his gaze, looking bashful. "I'm sorry I doubted you before."

Caw shrugged, feeling awkward. But after the rush of the moment had passed, the seriousness of what lay ahead hit him full force. "Now," he said, "how do we find Jawbone and the others?"

Crumb looked up and down the platform. The two pigeons he'd left at the ends of the street flew to him, calling softly.

"Not yet," he said. "We didn't come all this way just to practice."

A pigeon hopped up and down impatiently in front of him and warbled.

"As long as it takes, Bobbin," said Crumb.

Just then, two brown mice came scurrying along the platform. As Pip bent down to scoop them up, another hurried beneath Caw's feet. Pip placed them all on his shoulders. One of the tiny rodents lifted its snout to his ear.

Pip's eyes lit up. "They're coming," he said.

"Who's com—" Caw began. But as he spoke, he felt a presence at his back and spun around.

A bent old woman with a stick was walking in their direction, dragging one foot a little. She wore rubber Wellington boots and several layers of clothes. A gingham shawl covered her head, but a few white hairs had sprung free. Something was wrong with her eyes—they swiveled in their sockets, pointing in different directions like she couldn't decide which way to look. Caw relaxed. She might be crazy, though probably not much of a threat.

But as he turned back to Crumb, his heart jolted. Three more figures had emerged at the other end of the platform. One was a young, slightly built black man in a sharp business suit and dark sunglasses, carrying a briefcase. He clutched a newspaper under his arm, and Caw saw his own face on the folded front cover. Caw backed away, behind Crumb.

"Don't run," said the pigeon talker firmly. "You don't want to spook them."

Beside the suited man came a young woman, maybe early twenties, in a wheelchair. Rich brown curls fell on either side of a delicate, striking face with eyes that rose upward in the corners. She was being pushed by a muscular, square-jawed man wearing a coverall, like he'd just come from a building site. His brown hair was going gray at the edges, and his hands, Caw noticed, were huge and powerful. The four newcomers converged silently on Caw, Pip, and Crumb.

"Is this all?" said the pigeon talker. "I'd hoped for more."

Pip shrugged. "I sent loads of mice," he said. "Quaker said he'd had enough after what happened at his house. I guess he was afraid—maybe the others were too."

The disabled girl raised a hand in greeting, and from the open neck of her coat two squirrels emerged tentatively, one red, one gray. One went around her back and sat on her shoulder, while the other took a perch on the arm of her chair. They glared at Caw.

"She's a feral!" Caw gasped.

"They all are," muttered Crumb.

Caw turned to the old lady just as three giant centipedes, each three feet long and as thick as Caw's finger, scurried over her coat. Two disappeared back down her sleeves and the third shot into her Wellington boot.

Hmm, tasty, said Screech, clicking his beak.

Caw couldn't see any animals on either of the two men. Then the suited one stooped, laid down his briefcase, and popped open the lid. A swarm of bees rose in a spiral into the air. Caw felt a grin spreading over his lips.

"Thank you for coming," said Crumb.

"Why have you brought us here?" said the man pushing the wheelchair, in a gruff voice. He sounded irritated, maybe even angry. Caw's eyes swept over his body, wondering if any creatures were lurking in his clothes.

"You know why, Racklen," said Crumb. "You must have sensed it."

"We both did," said the man, turning his head slightly. Caw followed his gaze, and his heart gave a sudden jolt. Along the platform, lurking in the shadows, a large gray form crouched. He'd never seen a wolf in the city before. Its yellow eyes examined them, and then it padded out of sight.

"The Spinning Man," said the girl in the wheelchair, snapping Caw's attention back to the others.

"That's right, Madeleine," said Crumb. "How are you, by the way?"

The girl's squirrels cocked their heads, their noses twitching. Caw wasn't sure, but he thought he saw something in the look Crumb shared with her—a fondness. They must be about the same age, he guessed.

"I *was* doing fine," she said. "Until this morning."

The bee feral waved a hand, and his swarm zipped around him like a mini hurricane. "We've all seen his signs, Crumb. But the Spinning Man is dead and gone."

Crumb nodded. "Even so, his followers are loose in the city," he said. "And . . . now they have the Crow's Beak."

The assembled ferals all shifted and glanced at one another nervously. It was the centipede feral who spoke first. The old woman's voice was cracked and weak, but her eyes were full of fire. "The Crow's Beak is a useless artifact," she said. "There's no crow talker to wield it now that poor Lizzie is dead."

Lizzie, thought Caw, his heart lurching. *My mother.*

Crumb laid a hand on Caw's shoulder.

"A crow talker lives, Emily," said Crumb. "Her son."

The centipede talker did a double take. "This boy—the crow talker?" she said.

"Impossible!" said the girl in the wheelchair.

The bee feral laughed. "Crumb, the Carmichael kid died along with his parents. This boy's fooling you and wasting our time. I need to get to court. See you around."

He sent his bees buzzing back into the briefcase and snapped it shut. Then he turned to go, as did the others. "Wait!" said Pip.

The bee feral shook his head. "Stay out of trouble, mouse talker," he said.

Pip looked at Caw. "Show them!" he said.

Caw drew his hands quickly to his chest. In seconds, four murders of crows swept up in spiraled black trails, each circling a feral. It took all Caw's concentration to hold them in shape, but it worked. The ferals stopped in their tracks, and the wolf talker stared at Caw, frowning. "Jack Carmichael?" he said.

"You can call me Caw," said Caw. He dismissed the crows with a wave of his hand, and they scattered away from the station.

The girl in the wheelchair—Madeleine—looked at Caw coldly. "It would be better if you *were* dead," she said. Her words cut him to the bone. "You're a liability." She turned her attention to Crumb. "Send him away from Blackstone forever. As long as you keep the boy safe, the Spinning Man has no hope of returning."

Anger swelled in Caw's chest. How dare they talk about him like he wasn't there? "I'm not going anywhere," he said.

Madeleine gripped the wheels and thrust herself forward, scooting right up to Caw's feet. "You think I was always like this?" she spat. "No—the Spinning Man put me in this thing."

Caw tried to hold her stare. "I'm sorry," he said. "I didn't know."

"You know nothing," she said, her voice softening a little.

Caw looked at Crumb. *We're losing them,* he thought. "Look, I might not have fought in the Dark Summer, but my parents did. We have to do *something*."

"That's the old Carmichael stubbornness for you," said Racklen, the wolf feral. "Your parents wouldn't run either, and look where it got them."

His words threatened to puncture Caw's resolve. "A few days ago, I didn't even know there were other ferals," he said. "But then I learned about the Dark Summer. We won then, didn't we?"

The wolf talker shook his head. "There were only losers in that war," he said.

"Please, we have to fight," said Caw. "The Spinning Man's followers have my friend—they think she's the crow talker, but she's not. She's just a girl."

"Then she is none of *our* concern," said the squirrel feral. She turned her chair away and wheeled back toward the end of the platform.

"Maddie's right," said the old woman. "Crumb, we defeated the Spinning Man, but you must know we can't do it again. There were more of us back then. We were younger and more powerful."

"I'm more powerful now," said Crumb. "I've been training."

The centipede talker gave him a pained look and reached for him with a wrinkled hand. "Crumb, you always were a brave boy," she said, "but please, don't ask this of me. You know well enough what I suffered." She began to choke back tears. "I lost my . . . my children." Her shoulders shook as Crumb embraced her, his chin resting on her head. After a few moments she gathered herself and dried her eyes with a handkerchief. "My line ends with me, Crumb." Her gaze shifted to Caw. "If you're sensible, crow talker, you will run away so you don't suffer the same fate." She let her hand trail across Crumb's cheek. "Look after yourself, Samuel," she said.

Crumb nodded and watched her go, followed by the wolf feral.

The bee feral still hadn't moved by the time she reached the end of the platform.

"And you, Ali?" said Crumb. "Will you help us?"

The bee talker pursed his lips, then pushed his sunglasses back up his nose and picked up his briefcase once more. "Crumb, we had some tough times back then, but it was different. The stakes were high. My swarm gave their lives in that war."

"The stakes are high now," said Crumb.

"Not the same, brother," said Ali. "The Crow's Beak—it's just a myth. The kind of thing that mad recluse Quaker goes in for. Who's to say it even works?"

He began to walk away as well.

"What if you're wrong?" asked Pip.

"I'll take that risk," said the bee talker, without looking back.

"Cowards!" shouted Pip. But the ferals drifted away as quietly as they had arrived.

"Sorry, Caw," said Crumb. "It looks like it's just the three of us."

Caw sighed, and suddenly every ache felt a little deeper and more painful than before.

"Four," said a woman's voice.

The early morning sun peeked over the edge of the platform, throwing dazzling light into Caw's eyes as a tall figure stepped from one of the derelict rail carriages.

She must have been watching all along, thought Caw, blinking to make out her face.

Crumb started, taking a step back and squinting. "Velma? Is that you?"

As the woman stepped forward into the shadow of the awning, Caw gasped. Her hair flowed loose and wild around her face, and her eyes seemed slightly pointed in the corners and more luminous than before. Her long coat was tailored to her body, deep orange and flecked with white. But the face was unmistakable.

"Hello, Caw," said Mrs. Strickham.

15

"But—" Caw began. "How did you—"

"You know each other?" said Crumb, frowning.

"You've grown up, Crumb," said Mrs. Strickham. "I wish we were seeing each other again under better circumstances."

Crumb, for once, seemed speechless. The look in his eyes was a mixture of awe and disbelief, like an astonished child.

"I heard you called a gathering." She was almost gliding toward them. "Given my current crisis, I thought it wise to attend."

Caw glanced guiltily at Crumb, who was shaking his head. "You're the last person I expected to see," said the pigeon talker. "I thought you had left the city for good."

Despite her severe expression, Mrs. Strickham's lip trembled. "They have my daughter, don't they?"

Crumb's frown turned to openmouthed shock. "Lydia is your—"

"Yes," said Mrs. Strickham. "When I saw she wasn't with you, I— I feared the worst. And it seems I was right. She knows nothing about my . . . past. She must be so frightened, I—" Mrs. Strickham's face began to crumple with grief, but she quickly composed herself.

"I mean to get her back," she said, her voice a low growl. "Whatever it takes."

"You're a feral," said Caw.

Mrs. Strickham turned her piercing gaze on him, and he felt a little like prey in the sight of a predator. "Yes, crow talker."

Caw could barely believe it. "It's my fault," he said finally. "They think Lydia is the crow feral. But it's me they wanted!"

"Lydia never did like doing as she was told," said Mrs. Strickham with a grim smile.

"We'll find her," said Pip, puffing out his chest.

"Ah, the mouse talker," said Mrs. Strickham, eyes falling on the mouse crawling up Pip's sleeve. "I knew your father, young man. You have his eyes." She paused, and Caw thought how utterly terrifying she looked—standing straighter than before, her loose red hair twisting like flames in the breeze. "He died bravely."

Pip's eyes filled with tears, but he quickly dashed them away. "I know," he said. "Crumb told me."

"So what now?" said Caw. "How do we find Lydia?"

Mrs. Strickham turned her sharp gaze on him. "If Jawbone was with them, we could try the old underground network beneath the city." She pointed along the tracks. "During the Dark Summer, he and his pack were said to hide out there."

"But the network goes on for miles," said Crumb. "Even if he is down there, how will we find him?"

"Maybe I can help," said Pip. The young boy paled as Crumb and Mrs. Strickham both turned to look at him. But Caw gave him a smile, and he rallied a little. "There are mice down there," he explained. "Lots of mice!"

"Can you call them?" asked Caw.

Pip nodded. He knelt on the platform, placing his hands flat on it, and closed his eyes. Caw hopped down onto the tracks and saw that they descended toward the circular mouth of a tunnel leading into blackness.

Nothing.

And then, at last, a small brown creature scurried from the mouth of the tunnel. It was followed by another, and another. Soon a whole tide of mice surged out, spilling from the sides of the tunnel and dropping from the roof.

The mice flowed past Caw's ankles and up onto the platform, gathering around Pip like a rustling brown carpet, all squeaking at him. The boy's eyes flicked open, and his face lit up with a grin.

"I've never summoned so many!" he said proudly.

"Jawbone," said Mrs. Strickham sternly. "Where is he?"

"Sorry," said Pip. He listened again and at last sat up. "They've seen a big man with a tattoo on his face," he said. There was no triumph in his voice—only a tremble of fear. "He's been coming and going, and he always has dogs with him. They'll lead us."

Caw's heart jumped at the thought of the evil feral so close by.

"Then what are we waiting for?" said Crumb. He leaped down onto the tracks.

They set out together. Pip led the way, a tide of mice running ahead, while more perched on his shoulders and arms and in folds of clothing. Mrs. Strickham came close behind, even more mice swarming around her feet. Caw's crows flew overhead and paused at the entrance to the tunnel. Even Milky didn't seem sure about flying inside.

Is this the best idea? asked Screech, glancing into the tunnel. *I mean—it's the enemy's turf, isn't it?*

Scared, Screech? asked Glum.

No! said Screech. *Just cautious, that's all.*

Well, I'm terrified, said Glum.

Milky silently ruffled his feathers.

Caw concentrated and summoned more crows, and when he turned, he was grateful to see a flock gathering at his back. From the pigeons mixed in with the crows, he guessed Crumb was thinking the same. They were heading into the unknown. . . .

"Just stay close," Caw told his crows.

"What about the trains?" asked Pip.

"This line hasn't been used for a decade," said Crumb. "But keep your wits about you. There's bound to be a few dangerous characters down there who won't want to be found."

As the darkness swallowed them, Caw strained his eyes, trying to pierce the shadows. If Jawbone really was here, who knew what traps he might have set up?

Mrs. Strickham gave a soft click with her tongue. Caw heard a light padding of feet, and a furry shape slipped among the mice, keeping pace at her side with its ears pricked. As his eyes adjusted to the gloom, he realized what it was. He remembered the orange creature slinking beside the bushes at the Strickhams' house the night of the disastrous dinner.

"You're the fox talker," he said.

The fox was joined by another, and it made a clicking sound back at Mrs. Strickham.

"You're right," she told the fox with a sly grin. "He *is* a little slow."

Caw blushed and was glad of the darkness.

"Why didn't you say before?" he asked.

Mrs. Strickham kept her gaze fixed straight ahead. "Because I value my privacy," she replied. "I suspected who *you* were from the moment I laid eyes on you, Jack. I didn't want my daughter being mixed up with other ferals. I suppose you thought me very rude."

"It's all right," said Caw.

"No, it isn't," she said. "Because I failed." She turned to face him as she walked. "Perhaps I was naive—I thought I could protect Lydia from the world of the ferals. . . . I wanted her to have a childhood, you see? Like a normal girl. My own mother denied me that. As soon as I was old enough to understand, I was playing with foxes. I knew from the age of four that one day I would have the gift myself."

"And Lydia has no idea?" said Caw.

Mrs. Strickham shook her head. "I was very careful. After the Dark Summer, I rarely communed with my foxes, even though we'd been through a lot together."

"That's an understatement," muttered Crumb from up ahead.

"I— I'm sorry Lydia got involved," said Caw.

"Yes, so am I," said Velma Strickham simply. She quickened her steps, striding ahead, and her foxes trotted to keep up.

I don't think she likes you very much, said Screech, half walking, half flying beside Caw.

"Don't worry about her," said Crumb, dropping back next to him. "She's always been a bit, er . . . aloof."

"She *hates* me," said Caw. "And I don't blame her."

"She was the same with me, at first," said Crumb. After a brief pause, he lowered his voice. "There's something you should know about Velma Strickham, by the way. It was she who finally killed the Spinning Man."

Pip gave a low whistle through the darkness.

Caw stared after Mrs. Strickham's silhouette, as she turned the corner. *So she avenged my parents' death.* That made it even worse— he owed her.

Gradually, his eyes could make out more of the tunnel ahead— the crumbling brickwork and the gray tracks penetrating the distance. No sign of anyone else, and no dogs lurking. Against the shuffles of their footsteps, he heard water dripping, the rustling of the mice, and the occasional flap of the birds' wings.

Perhaps Mrs. Strickham had a point. He'd been so glad to have a friend, he'd become selfish. He could have told Lydia to stay at the church while he went to Gort House. But he hadn't. Just like he'd been selfish getting Miss Wallace involved. He hadn't known then what they faced or the lengths to which his enemies would go.

He knew now, though, and he wasn't going to take any more risks with Jawbone and the others. Having a powerful feral like Lydia's mother at his side made him feel a lot better, even if they weren't exactly *friends*.

Mrs. Strickham stopped dead. "What's that?" she murmured.

Then Caw felt it too—a tingling through his feet.

"It feels like a train," said Pip nervously, glancing up and down the tunnel. "I thought this line wasn't running anymore."

"It isn't," said Crumb.

The vibrations grew by the second, and then two bright white lights swerved around the corner behind them.

"Run!" said Crumb.

Caw's crows overtook him, flying down the tunnel in the same direction as Mrs. Strickham. Caw shot after them, with Pip running at his side, mice scattering in all directions.

"This way!" called Lydia's mother. "There's a platform ahead."

Light swamped the tunnel, casting long shadows. The train's roar filled Caw's ears. He didn't dare look back. Instead, he watched the tracks flying by at his feet. If he tripped, that was it. Then he glanced up to see the tiled walls of the station and the platform at chest height. Lights flickered overhead. He leaped after Mrs. Strickham, and then he and Crumb pulled Pip up to safety. The train came thundering along the tracks behind him.

"Hide!" shouted Crumb.

Mrs. Strickham sprinted toward an old ticket booth, and they crouched behind it as the train's brakes screeched. There was a sign on the tiled wall, but Caw couldn't read it.

"Mason Street," whispered Pip, following his eyes.

"I don't understand," said Crumb. "There shouldn't be any power down here."

The train shunted to a halt at the platform, and the crows and pigeons alighted on its roof, out of sight. Caw couldn't see Mrs. Strickham's foxes anywhere.

"Someone must have rewired the electrics," she whispered. "And I think I know who."

With a hiss, the doors at the carriage opened. Two slavering dogs, ears pricked, stepped onto the platform. Jawbone followed, casting a dead-eyed stare left, then right.

"Wait here, boys," the dog feral murmured. "Won't need you where I'm going."

The dogs sniffed the air and growled. Jawbone raised his huge head, and his eyes narrowed. "Got a visitor, have we?" he said. "Show yourself!"

Caw's neck prickled as he crouched. Mrs. Strickham had closed her eyes as if she was concentrating hard. When they snapped open, he saw her determination. She started to straighten, ready for the fight. . . .

Without thinking, Caw lunged forward, throwing himself into the open ahead of her.

"Caw, get back!" she hissed.

But it was too late. The dogs turned in a flash, muzzles contracting over their teeth.

"Just you, runt?" said Jawbone, grinning.

"Where's Lydia?" said Caw. "What have you done with her?"

"The crow talker's safe where she belongs," said Jawbone. "Shame I can't say the same about you. Dinnertime, boys."

The two dogs rushed across the platform at astonishing speed. *Come to me, crows!* Caw willed. He threw an arm toward the dogs, and two dozen crows swept down from the train roof, with Glum, Screech, and Milky in the lead.

Jawbone grunted as the dogs skidded to a halt. The crows swerved and landed on the dogs' backs with ripping talons. The dogs went into a frenzy, rolling and leaping and snapping to throw their attackers off. Some crows scattered, others held on. One crow let out a dying wail as it was hurled from a dog's mouth into a wall.

Then the foxes came—nine or ten of them, snarling and growling, emerged from abandoned elevators at the platform's edge. They fastened their jaws over the dogs' legs, making them howl in pain.

Jawbone stumbled back, a look of panicked surprise on his brutal tattooed face.

Pigeons swept over him, driving him back still farther. They managed to lift him a few feet off the ground, then hurled him down onto the platform. Jawbone fell to his knees and started crawling toward the open doors of the train carriage. His dogs scampered off into the tunnel, pursued by yapping foxes and screeching crows.

"Stop him!" shouted Mrs. Strickham.

The dog feral had almost made it as far as the carriage, still covered by flapping, pecking, stabbing pigeons. He reached out an arm streaked with blood, just as the door slid shut with a sudden bang.

Jawbone groaned and rolled across the platform, scrabbling against the tiled wall and slamming into some sort of metal box. The rusted cover of the box fell open, exposing a mass of electrical wires and panels within. The pigeons didn't let up. Caw saw that Crumb's face was twisted with anger. He realized he was seeing a new side of Crumb: the veteran of the Dark Summer, fierce and vengeful.

A handful of mice scurried out from beneath the carriage and back across the platform toward their master.

"You did it! You shut the door!" said Pip as the mice climbed his legs. He turned to the others. "They gnawed through the wires."

Crumb advanced on Jawbone, lifting his hand. With a beating of wings, his pigeons rose from the convict's prone form.

Caw winced when he saw what the pigeons had done. Jawbone's face was covered in cuts and scratches, the blood dripping onto the platform. His hands were torn and bloodied too.

Mrs. Strickham seemed unaffected by the pitiful sight. As she approached, Jawbone pushed himself back against the wall. His eyes widened. He was afraid of her, Caw realized. "You!" said the dog feral. "You're the one who killed my master!"

"Where's my daughter?" shouted Mrs. Strickham. "What have you done with her?"

Jawbone's great brow furrowed as he frowned. "Your *what*?" he said.

"You know who I'm talking about!" said Mrs. Strickham. As she spoke, three growling foxes approached with menace.

Jawbone's frown deepened. "I don't . . . understand. You're the fox feral. She's not your daughter."

"You've got the wrong person," Caw said. "I'm the crow talker." Glum and Screech came to rest, one on each of his shoulders. "I'm the one you want."

Jawbone said nothing, but his eyes blazed with helpless rage.

One of the foxes clambered over the dog feral's chest and brought its muzzle close to his face.

"Last chance," said Mrs. Strickham. "Where is she?"

Caw felt cold. Was she serious? No matter what horrible things the man had done, Caw couldn't bear the thought of those foxes hurting him any more.

But before he could say anything, Jawbone lunged to one side, sending the fox sprawling. He got up to run but instantly stumbled and fell. Blindly, he reached out a hand to steady himself, and grasped the only thing he could—the mass of exposed wires inside the open metal box.

There was a loud popping sound, and Jawbone's twisted mouth opened in a silent scream. His body jerked rigid, the veins on his neck standing up like worms under his skin. Then smoke rose from his eye sockets and he slumped to the ground next to the signal box, head thumping onto the platform.

16

"Good riddance," said Mrs. Strickham.

Crumb stood silently, staring at the dog feral's dead body. Pip was shaking, and Caw put a hand across his shoulders. One question drummed in his brain.

"How can we find Lydia now?" he said.

"Search his pockets," said Mrs. Strickham.

Caw crouched slowly beside Jawbone's smoking corpse. The thought of touching the body made him shudder, but he didn't want to appear weak in front of the others. He felt the feral's jacket. "Nothing," he said.

"Check inside," said Lydia's mother.

But Jawbone's pockets held nothing but a vicious-looking knife, with a black hilt and a blade shaped like a sharpened fang. Mrs. Strickham hefted it. "This was Jawbone's weapon of choice during the Dark Summer. He must have come back here to get it. Funny—I never took him for the sentimental sort." She tossed the knife to the ground with a clatter.

Wait! said Screech, twitching his beak. *Look at his shoe. I see something shiny!*

Caw examined the bottom of Jawbone's black boot and saw a glint of silver there. He pried the object out of the rubber sole with his fingers. It was a silver sewing needle.

"Mamba had one of these at the library," Caw remembered. His heart hammered as he thought of what she'd used it for. "And look at the cuffs of his jeans!"

Crumb and Mrs. Strickham peered closer. A few multicolored threads were clinging to the cuffs of Jawbone's jeans.

"Needles and threads," Crumb mused. "Strange."

"Textiles," Mrs. Strickham murmured, frowning in thought.

One of her foxes barked twice.

"Exactly what I was thinking, Ruby," said Mrs. Strickham. "There's an old sewing factory in the industrial quarter. It's been abandoned for years—my husband is always hearing about police activity over that way. It would be a perfect place to hide."

Caw's skin crawled. The followers of the Spinning Man using a sewing factory as their headquarters. . . . It made a strange, creepy kind of sense.

"Do you think Lydia's there?" he asked. He couldn't believe how calm they were after what had just happened.

"Maybe," said Mrs. Strickham. "Or maybe not. But it's the only lead we have. Let's go."

She turned toward the exit.

"What about him?" said Pip quietly, pointing to Jawbone's body.

Mrs. Strickham didn't break her stride. "Leave him to the rats."

They found the dead feral's dogs meekly sniffing at the gates to the underground station, their tails tucked between their legs.

"They're harmless now," said Mrs. Strickham, stroking one of the beasts behind its ears. The metal shutter was locked, but Pip soon had it open with a set of lock picks he pulled from his coat.

Rain had started to fall while they were fighting in the subterranean world. It scoured the streets of Blackstone, as if the lead sky was emptying itself. The four ferals ran through the downpour, staying under cover when they could. On days like this, Caw would usually have pulled over the nest tarpaulin and tried to sleep, but he felt wired. His shock at the chilling brutality of the ferals slowly faded, until he was left thinking only of Lydia. What if she wasn't at the sewing factory? What then? He tried to ignore his doubts, but it wasn't easy.

There weren't many people around as they headed for the industrial quarter. Pip was reliving the battle with Jawbone for most of the way, blow by blow. His blond hair was plastered over his head by the rain, but he didn't seem to mind.

"Your foxes were awesome!" he said to Mrs. Strickham. "How many can you call at once?"

Mrs. Strickham carried an umbrella, and the water poured off its sides in a constant stream. "I'm not sure," she said.

"I bet you can summon loads!" said Pip.

"I've not had the need to for a long time," said Mrs. Strickham wearily.

"Leave Velma alone," said Crumb.

Pip went into a sulky silence.

They soon reached the low-rise buildings of the industrial quarter—dormant factories and vacant warehouses spread out around a grid of streets, with parking lots scattered in between. Weeds grew up from the alleyways between the buildings. Caw's crows flew on ahead. He'd told them to keep a lookout for anything suspicious—any snakes or cockroaches lurking in the shadows. Screech landed on a lamppost and shook droplets from his feathers. More rain trickled from his beak.

Caw jogged up until he was alongside Lydia's mother. Her face was expressionless, her eyes distant.

"Mrs. Strickham?" he asked.

She came out of her trance and waved a hand impatiently. "Velma," she said. "Since circumstances have forced us together, we may as well not be strangers."

Caw nodded but couldn't bring himself to actually call her by her first name. "Is it true," he went on haltingly, "that some ferals can transform themselves into their animals?"

"So they say," she said, directing her gaze forward. "Though I don't know of any alive who can."

"So . . . you can't?"

She turned to him again with a piercing stare. "No, I can't," she snapped. "And if I were you, I'd concentrate on Lydia and stop daydreaming about the sort of legends Felix Quaker spouts."

She stopped at a junction between two streets and gestured at a gray, windowless building. "We've arrived."

"We'll investigate," said Crumb. He glanced at Velma, who gave a tiny nod.

"You two must wait outside," said Lydia's mother.

"What?" said Caw.

"This is not your fight," said Mrs. Strickham. "These are our old enemies. And they have my daughter."

"My parents—" Caw began.

"Your parents were killed by the Spinning Man," said Crumb. "And as long as you do not wield the Crow's Beak, the Spinning Man cannot return. Do as Velma says."

"No!" said Caw. "You *need* us."

"He's right!" said Pip.

Crumb stepped forward and placed his hands on Caw's shoulders, looking into his eyes. "Caw, you aren't ready," he said. "Simple as that." He leaned closer and spoke in a low voice. "Besides, if I don't come back, I need someone to look after young Pip."

Caw wanted to argue, but he checked his frustration on the tip of his tongue. "Fine," he muttered.

When Crumb released him, Caw saw that they were surrounded by a dozen foxes and a flock of pigeons. The two adults made their way across the road, side by side.

"You're just going to let them go?" said Pip angrily.

"We'll keep a lookout," said Caw, every word an effort. "The Spinning Man might have other followers nearby."

Pip slumped against a wall.

Good decision, said Glum, landing beside him. *Let the experts handle this one. They'll find Lydia in no time.*

Crumb and Mrs. Strickham crept along the side of the textile building toward a metal door, their creatures melting through the shadows in their wake. The rain was easing up at last.

The next moment, they had vanished into the building.

"I can't believe we're sitting this out," said Pip. He seemed close to tears.

"We're not," said Caw. He began to follow in the footsteps of Crumb and Mrs. Strickham.

We're not? said Screech, springing into the air.

"Hold on!" said Pip, scurrying after him. "I thought—"

"I just didn't want an argument," said Caw. "There's no way I'm going to stay out here when Lydia's in danger."

Glum flapped past and landed on the road ahead. *Caw, you heard what Crumb said. This isn't—*

"There's no point talking about it," interrupted Caw. "My decision's made. You can sit it out if you want."

Glum sighed, then followed.

They reached the door, still ajar. It was dark inside. Caw slipped through, with Pip at his heels. As his eyes adjusted to the gloom, he made out hundreds of desks and chairs stretching into the distance. Each desk had a piece of machinery on top. Dust coated the floor, making the footsteps of Crumb and Mrs. Strickham easy to follow. Some of the machines still had pieces of material piled up beside them.

"Sewing machines," whispered Pip.

Milky, Screech, and Glum landed on the nearest tables. The vast room was so quiet Caw could hear the rustling of their wings.

Halfway along the room was an enclosed office built against the side of the factory. The floor was littered with papers, and there were mannequins standing against one wall, with material draped over them. Caw guessed that no one had worked here for a long time. Maybe not since the Dark Summer.

Footsteps in the dust led toward the far corner of the building. A few mice crawled along the edge of the wall nearby.

"Backup," said Pip gravely.

Caw smiled, though he couldn't imagine what help the tiny rodents would be. In the corner, he saw a set of spiraling metal steps leading downward into a basement.

"Can you hear that?" said Pip.

Caw cocked his head to listen. There was some sort of rhythmic sound coming from below. "It sounds like chanting," he said. He couldn't make out the words.

He descended the stairs, heart thumping, placing each foot with care.

Before Caw reached the bottom, a cacophony of howls and screeches filled the air. He rushed down into an empty corridor with light at the far end. The animal sounds grew louder, and he broke into a run. As he skidded to the end, he saw a set of double doors with small glass windows. The light and the horrible sounds were coming from the other side of them.

He crept closer and looked through.

The first thing he saw was a ring of foxes standing guard around Mrs. Strickham, hackles up and snarling, but hesitating, as though afraid to move forward. The pigeons were the same, flocked in a circle around Crumb.

Caw pushed the door open a fraction, taking care to remain hidden. He saw a large storeroom, surrounded by pallets and crates and lit by candlelight that reflected off silver air-conditioning chutes on the ceiling above. There was a soft gasp from behind as Pip joined him, peering through the crack in the door with wide eyes.

Mamba and Scuttle occupied the center of the room, standing several feet apart, unarmed as far as Caw could see. He caught his breath. Between them stood Lydia, holding the Crow's Beak and shivering. There was a hood over her head and neck. At her feet, on the floor, strange shapes were drawn in some thick black substance.

"Don't you dare hurt her!" said Mrs. Strickham.

"Mom?" said Lydia. "Mom, is that you?"

"Nice try, my dear," said Scuttle, "but we know she's not your mother. She's the stinking fox talker."

"Don't worry, Lydia," said Mrs. Strickham, her voice tight with anxiety. "Everything's going to be fine now."

Scuttle chuckled.

"I don't think so," said Mamba. "Not unless everyone does exactly what I say. First, let's get rid of those foxes, shall we?" She pointed to a large, open-sided crate. "In there will do."

Lydia's mother glanced desperately at her daughter, then at the animals at her feet. At a flick of her hand, the foxes ran without hesitation into the crate, pressing their bodies on top of one another to fit. Mamba strode to the crate and slammed the lid closed, trapping the foxes inside.

"Pigeons too," she said. "Out."

Crumb hesitated for just a moment before raising a hand. His pigeons took off, and Caw and Pip jerked back from the doors as the birds burst through them, flying past in a stream, then vanishing around the corner of the corridor. Cautiously, Pip pushed the door open again.

"Now," said Mamba, focusing her attention on Lydia. "Use the Crow's Beak."

"Do it, Lydia," said Mrs. Strickham. "Cut a hole in the veil!"

"I told them a thousand times already," said Lydia. "I don't know how. They keep calling me the crow talker! What are you *doing* here, Mom?"

She sounded frightened, her voice muffled beneath the hood.

Scuttle's feet shifted, and he cast a nervous glance at Mamba. "Enough!" hissed the snake feral. "We haven't come this far to be fooled by a stupid trick. We know your real mommy is long gone, crow talker. Now get on with it!"

"Mom, please, tell them the truth!" said Lydia. "Tell them I'm just a normal girl!"

"Listen to me, sweetheart," said Mrs. Strickham. "Do as the lady says. Hold the sword up and drag it from side to side."

"But—"

"Do it!" said Mrs. Strickham sharply.

Suddenly, Caw understood. *If Mamba and Scuttle realize Lydia's useless to them, they'll kill her in an instant.*

Mamba started chanting again under her breath.

"She's calling to him," whispered Pip, his eyes wide with fear. "Those shapes on the floor and that funny language—it's meant for talking to the dead. Crumb explained it to me once. She must be telling the Spinning Man to . . . to get ready."

Lydia waved the Crow's Beak. Nothing happened.

"Try again, Lydia!" said Mrs. Strickham. She took a step forward and Scuttle snapped his fingers, turning on her. Cockroaches swept from inside his clothes and across the floor, their shells clacking together. "Stop right there!" he said as the creatures swarmed into a circle around Crumb and Mrs. Strickham. "Or they'll strip your flesh from your bones."

"It's not working," hissed Mamba.

"Maybe the little grub was telling the truth after all," snapped Scuttle. "Maybe the fox talker really is her mother, which means—"

"The girl is just afraid," said Crumb, obviously trying to stall. "Give her another chance."

"We don't have time for this," said Mamba. She stepped toward Lydia, her eyes narrowing. Then she reached up and snatched the hood from Lydia's head.

"No!" gasped Mrs. Strickham.

Caw's heart stopped. Around Lydia's neck was a black snake, coiled tight. Its head rose a little, until it hovered beside her ear. Lydia flinched as its tongue flickered.

"This snake is only a baby," said Mamba, "but his bite will kill a whelp like you in less than a minute. You'll die like your dog, spasming in pain. By the time your father sees your body, it'll be puffed up so much he won't recognize you. The time for games is over. Cut the veil in the next three seconds, or my patience will run out. One . . ."

"Please," begged Mrs. Strickham.

"Two . . ."

"Don't do this," said Crumb.

"Three . . ."

Caw burst through the door, with his crows and Pip at his back. "Stop!" he shouted. "I'm the crow talker!"

"It's the scruffy kid from the library!" said Scuttle with a sneer. "But how can he—"

Mamba clenched a fist and punched her other palm. "Of course it's him!" she said. "He must have been at her house when the crows were waiting outside. When my snake killed the little dog."

Caw glanced at Mrs. Strickham, whose face was rigid with fear. If he could just distract them long enough, Lydia might get out of this alive. "Jawbone realized too," Caw said. "Before he died."

Scuttle jerked his eyes toward Mamba, then to Caw, blinking rapidly. "Dead?" he said. "You're lying."

"It's true," said Crumb. "Even a lump of meat like Jawbone can't withstand twenty thousand volts."

Scuttle narrowed his gaze, and the cockroaches around Mrs. Strickham and Crumb scurried as one to surround Caw. "Not scared, eh?" said the roach talker. "You should be. You'll be nothing but bones and scraps of clothing if I give the word. Your feathered friends can't do a thing about it."

"You need me," said Caw. "I'm the only one who can use the Crow's Beak."

"Caw, don't!" said Lydia. Mamba shot her a look, and Lydia gasped as the snake around her neck slithered a fraction tighter, its head bobbing from side to side. Lydia's eyes began to bulge as her face darkened.

"The poor girl can hardly breathe," said Mamba. "Any tighter and her blood vessels will start to pop."

Caw inched forward and the cockroaches went with him, edging him closer to his friend. With a jolt of horror he saw that the black shapes on the floor weren't painted. They were made out of spiders, hundreds of them, all sitting perfectly still. Together they formed a distorted circle with eight crooked legs.

"Let her go," said Caw desperately.

"You know what we want," said Scuttle. "You hold the key."

Caw looked at Mrs. Strickham and Crumb. The pigeon talker's jaw was clenched. Mrs. Strickham let her eyelids slowly close, either in resignation or because she couldn't bear to look. What did that mean? What was he supposed to do?

"All right!" said Caw. "I'll open the door to the Land of the Dead. Just release her, please!"

"Cut the veil, and *then* we let her go," said Mamba.

"No," breathed Crumb. "He must not come back."

"There's no choice," said Caw. "It's the only way."

He glanced at Mrs. Strickham. Her eyes were open again, and the emotions fought in her face.

"If he returns, we're all dead," said Crumb, staring pleadingly at Lydia's mother. He looked like a little boy, utterly terrified.

The pigeon talker's right, said Glum. *You can't.*

Listen to Glum, Caw. Please, said Screech.

Caw looked to Milky for guidance. The pale bird said nothing, but something in his eyes gave Caw courage—and seemed to tell him that the choice he had already made in his heart was the right one.

As Caw reached the circle of spiders, the cockroaches stopped, as if they were afraid to pass through. Caw stepped into the circle and felt a twinge of nausea in his stomach, like the world had tilted a little.

"Give me the Crow's Beak, Lydia," said Caw. No matter what the cost, he couldn't let Lydia die. He had to save her.

"Caw, don't do this," said Crumb. "You weren't there eight years ago. You can't understand what you're doing."

Mrs. Strickham was silent, chin slightly raised in defiance but skin desperately pale.

Lydia's face was wet with tears as she handed the Crow's Beak to Caw. Her eyes fixed on his, round with fear. As his fingers closed over the cold leather, Caw was surprised by how light the blade felt—it might have been a switch of willow rather than metal. It fitted his hand perfectly.

"That's it," said Mamba as the snake's coils loosened on Lydia's throat.

"Stand in the center," said Scuttle.

"Caw, stop!" shouted Crumb angrily. "In the name of your parents, put down the Crow's Beak."

Lydia glanced back and forth between Caw and her mother. Mamba had begun to chant again.

The three crows swept unsummoned across the room. Glum and Screech suddenly backed away, hissing.

We can't cross! said Glum.

Caw, come out of there! called Screech.

Only Milky landed on his shoulder.

"Come to keep me company?" said Caw.

Milky blinked, and Caw saw himself reflected in the crow's pale eye.

Caw lifted the Crow's Beak. "Remember our deal," he said to Mamba.

He moved the sword through the air, feeling a slight resistance as if he were slicing through cloth. A sudden chink of blinding light made him turn away.

"It's working!" said Scuttle. "Keep cutting!"

To his side, Caw saw that Crumb was openmouthed. Even Mrs. Strickham was trembling.

"I'm sorry, Caw," said Lydia. "I'm so sorry."

He dragged the Crow's Beak in a curve. Squinting into the flooding light, he couldn't see anything beyond the bright irregular doorway.

"Now step back," hissed Mamba, her face alive with excitement. "The portal will only last for a few moments."

Caw took a step away, then felt a tugging at his hand. Caw turned to see Lydia next to him. "You've saved me too many times already," she murmured, her voice strangled and hoarse. "It's my turn to save you."

"Lydia . . . ," said Mrs. Strickham, her voice urgent.

Before Caw realized what was happening, Lydia had snatched the Crow's Beak from him and leaped into the portal, the snake still wrapped around her neck.

"No!" Mamba screamed. In a split second, the portal zipped closed, the candles flickered out, and all the spiders at Caw's feet scuttled away, disappearing into the shadows.

Lydia was gone.

17

Caw slumped to the ground in shock. The air was suddenly cold, and through the noise in his head he could hear Velma Strickham sobbing. When he looked up, Mamba was on her knees moaning, hands clasped to her scalp. Scuttle was staring at the place where the portal had been, shaking his head and muttering, "No, no, no . . ."

"Why?" said Mamba. "Why would she do that?"

To stop the Spinning Man from returning, thought Caw. *Without the Crow's Beak, no one can come back. Not even Lydia.* It felt like someone had scooped out his heart and replaced it with lead. *She sacrificed herself to save us.*

"Why didn't you stop her?" Mamba screeched at the roach talker.

"Why didn't *you?*" Scuttle snapped. "Wretched brat took the Crow's Beak with her!"

"You're the one who was blabbing on about the Land of the Dead in front of the girl all this time," Mamba shot back at the hunchbacked man. "If it wasn't for you, she never would have gotten it in her head to do this!"

"What difference does it make?" said Crumb. "It's over."

Mamba's eyes flashed onto him. "Not so fast, pigeon talker," she said. Her long fingers twitched and several snakes slithered from the crates at the edge of the room, making straight for Crumb and Mrs. Strickham. Another headed for Pip.

Crumb threw out his hand, and two pigeons appeared from the dark corners of the room. They swooped down at the snake nearest Pip. But the snake flailed, catching one pigeon in its jaws and rolling its coils over the second.

"Run, Pip!" said Crumb. Wriggling snakes were backing the pigeon talker into a corner. The mouse feral made for the door, pausing only to let a clutch of mice scurry from his trouser legs. But the next instant a tide of cockroaches went after him, smothering the mice easily as Pip fled the room.

Caw saw Mrs. Strickham kick one snake aside and stamp on another, before leaping up onto a stack of crates. Her tear-filled eyes scanned the room. She pushed over one of the crates, crushing more snakes, then leaped off onto the floor, running for the same exit as Pip. The crate of foxes shook as the animals inside growled and snarled, powerless to help their mistress.

Caw scrambled to his feet and ran too, only to feel a sharp blow to the back of his neck that sent him tumbling and seeing stars. Through the pain he willed his crows to leave.

We won't leave you, said Screech, flapping above the melee.

"Go!" Caw shouted. "Do as I say!"

Finally the three crows flew out of the room.

As he lay on the ground, trying to shake his head clear, Caw saw cockroaches approaching, just inches from his nose. Their jaws twitched hungrily.

"No sudden moves," said Scuttle, standing over him.

Caw placed his hands carefully by his shoulders and pushed himself upright, staggering a little. Crumb was pressed against a wall, utterly trapped by Mamba's hissing snakes and hundreds of Scuttle's creatures.

The two pigeons that had tackled the snake were both on their backs, surrounded by broken feathers. One was dead already, while the other's legs twitched in its death throes.

"Shall we kill them now?" said Scuttle.

Mamba glared at Caw, her face dark with anger. After a couple of seconds, she shook her head. "Not yet," she said. "Maybe there's another way. . . . The crow talker might still be able to help us, whether he likes it or not. Take them to the repair room while I think this through."

Scuttle snapped his fingers and the creatures at Caw's feet moved as one, forcing him toward the doors. Crumb followed, surrounded by the snakes. If either of them made a move, the other would die for certain. There was no escape. At least Pip and Mrs. Strickham seemed to have gotten away.

The roach feral led them to a door off the main corridor. Inside was a small, windowless room, lit only by a dim, naked bulb and filled with broken sewing machines piled on top of one another.

"Sit tight," said Scuttle with a grin. "We're off to catch your friends." The snakes and the cockroaches left the room, and the door slammed closed. Caw heard a key turn in the lock.

"What now?" he said.

Crumb leaned back against the wall and slumped down until he was sitting with his knees bent. He looked weary. "I'm sorry, Caw," he said. "But we're done for."

Caw's blood was still pumping from the fight. He wasn't going to give up. Not while Lydia was trapped in the Land of the Dead. Plus, Mrs. Strickham and Pip had escaped—they might be able to figure something out together. He scanned the room. "Maybe we can pick the lock."

"Mamba's not stupid," said Crumb. "There'll be thirty deadly snakes outside that door."

Caw felt a surge of anger, but before he could reply there was a soft tickle on his hand. He looked down and saw a small, delicate spider crawling up his wrist. He brushed it away, and it dangled for a moment on a slender thread from the ceiling. Caw followed the silk upward. There—a loose ventilation grille, high up and opposite the door.

When he looked down again, the spider was gone.

Heart thumping, he threw aside the carcass of a sewing machine and climbed up onto the workbench. Even at full stretch, his hand was still an arm's length from the grille. He bent his knees and jumped, but fell a fraction short. He tried again with the same result.

"Get up and give me a boost," he said.

Crumb grunted. "Why?"

Caw's anger swelled. "We can't just sit here!" he said.

"Velma and Pip are our only hope," said Crumb. He looked crumpled—defeated. "And that's a long shot. Save your energy for when Scuttle comes back. At least we can die fighting."

"But Lydia's in danger!"

Crumb fixed his gaze on Caw's, and for a moment, a fire had returned to his eyes. "She's not in danger," he said. "She's dead." His words rocked Caw back on his heels, and Crumb added more softly, "Or as good as. The Spinning Man has her. She took the Crow's Beak with her, so there's no way back. Only the crow talker can wield it. Besides . . . open your eyes, Caw." He pointed upward. "That vent is less than two feet across and half as high. You won't fit."

Caw looked up at the vent. Crumb was right—it was too small for him.

"But not for a crow," he murmured.

"What's that?" said Crumb.

"A crow could fit through that vent," he said.

"I can't see a crow," said Crumb, his voice a little shrill. "And even if you somehow managed to summon one through the other side, *you're* still locked in here." His eyes softened. "Caw, I'm sorry."

Caw jumped down from the workbench, feeling oddly light-headed. "What if I *was* a crow?"

Crumb waved a hand dismissively. "I told you, kid—even with a lifetime of practice, you wouldn't be able to do it. Trust me, I've tried."

"But *I* haven't," said Caw. Crumb rolled his eyes, and the gesture only made Caw more determined.

"Knock yourself out," said the pigeon talker.

Caw turned away from Crumb and sat in the middle of the floor, cross-legged. A couple of days ago, he'd never have thought it possible to summon crows to him, let alone get them to carry him. He closed his eyes and concentrated, remembering the strange feeling of lightness he'd felt at Felix Quaker's house, when he stared into Milky's eyes and drifted into the bird's consciousness.

He focused on that feeling, let Crumb's breathing fade into the background, and imagined Milky's eye—the way he had let himself sink into its bottomless . . .

"Any luck?" asked Crumb.

"Quiet!" said Caw.

He concentrated again, and after a few seconds felt the pull once more. A tingle of energy crept slowly along the lengths of his arms, as if the blood in his veins was suddenly a degree or two warmer. It was the same feeling he'd had back at the nest when he'd summoned the crows from all corners of the park—a latent power, just waiting to be unleashed. But this time, Caw didn't want to unleash it. He wanted to use it on himself. To turn it inward. He took a deep breath and, as he did, focused on drawing the energy back along his arms and into his chest. The temperature of his blood rose again, becoming uncomfortable.

"It can't be," muttered Crumb, his voice distant.

Caw gritted his teeth. Whatever was flowing beneath his skin, flooding his veins, it felt more like fire than blood. Every nerve ending screamed for him to stop, and every second that he didn't the pain grew worse. A rolling ball of agony built in his chest, and each breath made it more molten. All that existed was the pain, rolling tighter and tighter, leaving the rest of his body insubstantial. At any point he could release it, but if he did it would all be for nothing. Lydia needed him. He pressed the pain down by force of will, kept it from escaping.

From a faraway place, Crumb's voice called, "Don't stop! You're doing it!"

Caw's face felt as if it was floating away.

He couldn't feel his legs, and his bones seemed almost hollow. His arms felt impossibly powerful, as if he could lift whole buildings.

It was time. He exhaled and the power rushed through him, leaving his fingertips, then his hands, then sweeping back along his arms until they were weightless.

He moved them up and down . . .

. . . and felt his body rise.

When Caw opened his eyes, he was in the air, looking down at Crumb. The world seemed curved, and Caw realized he could see *behind* himself as well. The pigeon talker's mouth was hanging open. "Caw?" he said.

Caw laughed, and heard his own voice as a crow's raucous cry.

I've done it!

With a couple of flaps he rose to the air vent and attacked it with his beak, tearing the loose grille away and sending it clattering to the ground. Cool air rushed in, ruffling his feathers. Casting a last glance at Crumb, who was slack-jawed with wonder, Caw swept out of the room and into the sky.

It was *effortless*. Just a thought and his wings carried him upward. Caw soared above the factory, and Blackstone swept into view through a haze of falling rain. He climbed and climbed until he could see the hills to the west and the Blackwater vanishing into the fields of the east. He cocked his head and saw the sprawling buildings and the square patch of the park beside the prison. The world—his old life—seemed so small.

With a twitch of his wings, he veered and dived, gliding, buffeted by the rain. He tilted over the corrugated roofs of the industrial quarter, then looped between the steel cabling of a bridge over the river. Cars followed their rigid straight tracks, splashing through puddles beneath him.

Caw put on a burst of speed, amazed at how quickly he flew. His body was powerful and light at the same time, and the air gave way to his wishes as if they were one.

The next moment there were three more crows flying with him, two black and one white.

Caw? said Screech. *Is that you?*

It's me! Caw told him. *I'm one of you now.*

I don't believe it! said Glum.

I always knew he could do it, said Screech. *Always said he was special, didn't I?*

Milky blinked slowly, as if he wasn't surprised at all, then flapped forward, flying out in front. Without saying anything, the white crow led them north through the rain-swept sky. For a while Caw thought they were flying back toward the nest. He increased his wing speed and overtook Glum and Screech.

Show-off! said Glum.

Caw drew up alongside Milky. *Please*, he said. *I need you to tell me how to cross into the Land of the Dead. There has to be another way.*

Milky cocked his head slightly.

I mean it! said Caw. *You've been there—you know!*

Milky tipped his wings and flew northeast.

Where are we going? called Screech.

I have no idea, said Glum.

Is that a yes? asked Caw, tracking Milky.

But the white crow simply flew.

It wasn't long before Milky began to descend. They were right on the edge of Blackstone, then over fields, flying low toward a clutch of houses around a cemetery beyond. Caw stared in wonder at the landscape unfolding beneath his wings.

Milky flew along a lane leading up to a wrought-iron gate. The green, rolling hills of the cemetery within were crowded with headstones of all shapes and sizes. Milky circled once, then came to rest on one—a wet, gray slab of marble, leaning slightly and surrounded by puddles and weeds.

Caw landed, hopping on springy crow legs, and wondered how he was supposed to return to his human form. He concentrated hard, as he had done before, and focused on releasing that power he had worked so hard to build. It was surprisingly easy compared to his first transformation, like exhaling a deep, deep breath. Within moments, he was himself again. His body felt leaden and unwieldy, all gangly, unbalanced limbs. His coat was soaked. He staggered and put his hand on a gravestone. After a couple of breaths, normality returned.

"What is this place?" he asked, as he scraped damp hair from his eyes. An idea already lurked at the edges of his consciousness, but he shied away from it.

Milky tapped one foot on the marble slab.

Caw couldn't read the words, but as he crept closer, he recognized one thing clearly enough. Engraved in the stone was a picture of a crow. A lump formed in his throat. "This is my parents' grave, isn't it?"

It is, said Milky, his ancient voice a whisper. *Graveyards are special places, where the tissue between this land and the other is at its thinnest.*

Someone's feeling chatty! said Glum.

Caw laid a hand on the cold stone. Who had buried his parents here? he wondered. Felix Quaker? Or another feral, some ally from the war of the Dark Summer?

Caw felt tears prick in his eyes as he thought about his mother and father. But after a moment, he dashed them away. He didn't have time for questions or for sadness. He had to save Lydia.

"How do I cross?" Caw asked.

You must harness the power of the crows, said Milky, *and ask their permission.*

Caw's heart quickened. Even without the Crow's Beak, there was a way.

He closed his eyes and called his crows to him. He imagined himself high above the tiny graveyard, above the village. He reached out across Blackstone, drawing crows into the channels of his energy, feeling his connection to each and every bird as if they were linked by an invisible thread.

And they came. One by one, then in flocks of larger and larger sizes. The gray sky filled with black spots drifting steadily toward the graveyard. They alighted on the gravestones, along the iron gate, on the roofs of marble crypts guarded by statues of angels. They jostled for position on the grass, feathers rubbing against feathers, a carpet of black. Caw gaped in astonishment.

But what now?

Speak to them, said Milky, as if he could hear Caw's thoughts.

Caw shoved his hands into his pockets so no one would see that they were shaking, and he called out over the assembled crows.

"Thank you for obeying my summons," he said. The crows watched him with their beady eyes, and he felt his confidence falter under their critical gaze. "I am Caw, the crow talker, and this is the grave of my mother, the crow talker before me. Most of you don't know who I am. But I have brought you here for a special reason." He paused and took a deep breath. "I must travel to the Land of the Dead."

A thousand crow voices assaulted Caw's ears, and though it was hard to make out all the words, the tone was clear. *Never . . . Impossible . . . Danger . . . Mad . . . Fool.*

Caw glanced at Milky, who lifted his beak a fraction.

"Are there any crows here who fought in the Dark Summer?" said Caw.

A smattering of squawks.

"You fought for my mother, alongside other ferals," said Caw. "And why?"

For our lives, said a huge crow near Caw's feet. Caw noticed he had only one leg, and his beak was broken off halfway, its edges blunted.

"Just for your lives?" said Caw, "Or maybe for Blackstone—the city that has always harbored you and your families, your ferals. Maybe because it was the right thing to do."

The warrior crow was silent. Caw began to feel his confidence return.

"Your bravery helped banish the Spinning Man to the Land of the Dead. But he is still not defeated. He has my friend."

Our job is to protect you, said Glum softly.

"And I must protect Lydia," said Caw. "We can't always run and hide. The Spinning Man's disciples will not stop until he returns, one way or another."

He is trapped there, said a wiry female crow. *We are safe.*

I'm losing them, thought Caw desperately.

"Lydia is not just my friend," he said. "She is the daughter of the fox talker."

A murmur of surprise spread among the crows, and several

bobbed their heads and shot looks at their companions. Caw sensed the shift in mood. "That's right!" he said. "Lydia is the daughter of the one who banished the Spinning Man to the other side. We owe it to Velma Strickham to rescue her daughter."

Is this true? asked the female crow, glancing at Caw's crows.

'Fraid so, said Screech, with a nonchalant tip of his wing.

"Will you help me?" asked Caw. "For my mother, who died by his hand, and for the fox talker, who saved you from him?"

The crows fell silent, considering his words.

The old warrior crow was the first to jump into the air, then the others followed, their wingtips brushing Caw's shoulders. They each flew away from the graveyard, their bodies stretching away into a black ribbon through the sky.

"No," breathed Caw. He threw a desperate glance at Milky. "They can't go!"

Milky, Screech, and Glum took off as well without a word and joined the departing crows. Caw fell to his knees beside his parents' grave, resting his head on the stone.

"I'm sorry," he said, unsure whether he was talking to them, to Lydia, to Mrs. Strickham, or to himself. "I tried."

As he crouched there, despair gnawing at his heart, the air stirred around him, and Caw felt a wind tug lightly at his coat. He jerked up and saw the murder of crows swooping overhead. They had returned. The birds formed into a column of swirling feathers.

What was happening?

The spiral tightened as the crows flew in faster and faster circles, until Caw could no longer make out individual birds among the swarm. They began to descend toward him, a solid, spinning cylinder of black. Caw's clothes and hair whipped in the current. He was scared and exhilarated as the column closed around him, blocking out all but a circular patch of sky above.

He felt his feet leave the ground as the birds flew faster still. He couldn't tell whether it was night or day any longer, and then he lost his bearings completely—up, down, left, and right meant nothing. He held out his arms and lifted his chin, giving himself up to the rush of feathers.

Something gripped his weightless body, and the blackness overcame him completely.

18

Silence fell suddenly, as if a door had slammed shut on the sounds of the world. Caw opened his eyes and found himself standing in swaying meadow grass that reached his knees. Wisps of gossamer clouds stretched across a blue sky. Ahead the ground rose slightly to a woodland of astonishing green, its leaves rustling lightly.

Caw glanced around, narrowing his eyes into hazy sunshine. More fields lay in that direction, stretching all the way to the horizon. He'd never seen anything so beautiful. The clean air swelled his lungs and made him sigh with contentment.

All the crows had vanished, except one.

We have arrived, said Milky.

The pale old crow was sitting on his shoulder, but something had changed.

"Your eyes!" said Caw.

The cloudy film of blindness from the real world had lifted. Milky's eyes were black orbs, reflecting Caw's face back at him.

In the Land of the Dead, my vision returns, said the crow.

"Where to now?" asked Caw.

Milky rose and flew toward the forest. Caw followed, trampling down the grass in long strides. All the way, the sun warmed his back. He hadn't imagined the Land of the Dead would be like this. He felt like lying down and letting it wash over him. The soft grass would be a perfect place to rest, cushioning his body. He could think about other things later. . . .

Lydia. An urgent voice broke through from deep within his mind.

Caw shook his head to clear it. That's why he was here—to find his friend.

Milky was waiting on a low branch at the forest's edge. As Caw entered the shadowy world beneath the emerald canopy, more crows swooped between the twisting branches, curving past gnarled trunks toward him. They were all white like Milky—they came like snowflakes sucked on a powerful current of air and alighted on the branches above until they formed a semicircle with Caw at the center.

Welcome, Milky, they said as one, their voice a deep murmur that seemed to come from the air and the ground at the same time. *And welcome, Milky's friend.*

"Hello," said Caw, giving them a wave. "I'm Caw."

We know who you are, crow talker, said the crows. *You are not the first to cross the borders. The question is why you have come.*

Caw looked to Milky, then spoke. "I've come to save my friend from the Spinning Man," he said.

The crows began to bob and cock their heads, warbling softly to one another, then fell silent.

They have agreed to be your guides, Caw, said Milky.

Follow us, said the crows. *We will take you where you need to go.*

The white flock took off and flew ahead, each landing a few feet beyond the next, forming a pale path through the forest. Caw followed their trail beneath the rustling foliage. The ground was soft with moss and grass and tiny flowers—a paradise.

"What is this place?" he asked.

This is the land in its truest form, said Milky, *before the city of Blackstone was founded.*

"But where is everyone?" asked Caw. "If this is the Land of the Dead, where are they?"

The dead are all around you, said Milky. *After a time, their souls become part of the forest, just as in your world a body degrades into its elements.*

"But not everyone," said Caw. "Not the Spinning Man."

In the end, everyone fades, said Milky. *But there are some who take longer than others—those who retain a powerful emotional link with your world. Hatred. Love. Longing. Some even grow stronger for a time, if their desire is great enough. Look closer, and you can see them.*

Caw glanced around, into the gloom where the darkness

swallowed the receding trees. Sure enough, in the corners of his eyes he saw shapes drifting and flitting between the trunks. But each one appeared only for a moment before it was gone. He felt a shiver of unease, and an ache of sadness pressed on his heart.

The path of crows ceased at the base of a huge tree, with several birds perched on its exposed roots. There was something familiar about the shapes in the bark. . . .

"It's my tree!" said Caw. "From the park. What's it doing here?"

The Land of the Dead mirrors our own, said Milky, *sometimes in unexpected ways.*

Caw's eyes followed the trunk upward and saw his nest built into the branches above. His heart felt a sudden pang, then a heaviness.

He reached up for the familiar handholds, but Milky's squawk made him look around.

We should go on, he said. *Remember why we're here.*

Caw frowned, his mind foggy, as he struggled to understand the crow's words. He remembered dimly that it had been hard to get here, but he wasn't sure why. "I've got to look," he said. "I won't be long."

It's easy to become lost in the Land of the Dead, said Milky.

"Just a couple of minutes," said Caw. "The crows led me here, remember."

Milky said nothing.

Caw climbed quickly, feeling stronger than ever. He sensed the nest drawing him upward, reeling him closer. He longed to reach it like never before. The crows became smaller and smaller on the ground below, like scattered snowdrops among the lush grass. As he reached the bottom hatch, he paused with his hand on the plastic. Something was waiting inside for him, he realized. Something important.

He wasn't scared as he pushed his head through.

His breath locked up in his throat and time seemed to stop. A low table held three steaming cups and a cake on a chipped plate, already missing a few slices. But it was the two people sitting at either side who held Caw's rapt gaze.

"Hello, son," said his father, eyes crinkling at the corners.

"Jack!" said his mother, her lips stretching into a huge smile. "You're here at last! We missed you so much."

Caw's eyes flooded with sudden hot tears. "Mom? Dad?"

"Please, come in," said his father. "Join us."

They were really here, close enough to touch, looking relaxed and dressed in the same clothes as in his dream—his mother's black dress, his father's casual trousers and open shirt. Their smell, so comforting and familiar, filled the nest.

But Caw hesitated. The old anger, stewing for so long, bubbled to the surface. How dare they act just like nothing had happened, as if they'd been waiting for him all this time? "You left me," he said. "You *left* me. I was five years old, and you just sent me away!"

His parents shared a pained glance, as if they'd been expecting this reaction. His mother took a deep breath and then looked at him with her round, dark eyes, holding his tearful gaze with her own. "Believe me, it was the most painful moment of our lives," she said. "The agony of losing our son was worse than all that followed."

"We had no choice, Jack," said his father.

"Yes, you did," said Caw. "You let me think you didn't care. You could have told me."

"Told you that we were about to be killed?" said his mother, her strong voice reminding Caw of Velma Strickham's. "When you were five? Think hard, Jack—would you have wanted to know that while you were growing up? Would it have helped?"

Caw looked down, lost in thought. "It would have been better than knowing nothing at all," he said, but as the words left his mouth, he realized they probably weren't true.

"I knew the crows would look after you," said his mother. "The last thing I asked of them was that they should never tell you what had happened. I worried that you would try to find the Spinning Man."

"We just wanted you to be safe," said his father. "We hoped—prayed—you might forget."

"Well, I didn't," said Caw. How could anyone forget being carried away by crows from their bedroom window? "I dreamed about it every night."

"We're so sorry, Jack," said his mother. "You didn't deserve this."

As a single tear dropped from his mother's eye, Caw's heart softened. He saw it now: their decision to send him away hadn't haunted only his life—it had haunted theirs, even in death.

His anger drained, leaving him empty. The past was done, and now he had a chance to speak to the parents he thought he'd lost. He climbed slowly into the nest. "We can be together now," he said. "A family again."

Milky landed on the corner of the nest. *We came here for a reason, remember?*

Caw shot the old white bird an irritated glance. What was he talking about?

"Just leave me with my family," he said. He reached for one of the china cups, but his mother intercepted his hand. Hers passed through his like the touch of the softest silk.

"Milky's right, Jack," she said, wiping the tears from her face. "The Land of the Dead is not your home."

"Why not?" said Caw. "I like it here."

"You still have more to do with your life," said his father. "Your friend—Lydia—she needs you."

"Lydia?" said Caw. The name meant something, but he couldn't put his finger on what.

"The Spinning Man has her," said Caw's mother. "You are the

only chance she has." She reached up and laid a hand against his cheek. "Remember?"

At her delicate touch, Caw's brain shook loose the clouds that filled it. "Lydia!" he said. "Of course!" How had he forgotten her?

He let his cheek rest against his mother's palm, but he couldn't feel anything. And now that he looked harder at her, he saw she wasn't truly there at all. Neither was his father. Their bodies were like a mist, insubstantial and fleeting. A sharp wind and they'd be blown away. What was it that Milky had said? That those with a powerful emotional link to the living world took longer to vanish. Was that what was keeping his parents here—their connection with him? Their guilt at leaving him behind?

His parents were both smiling at him, a little sadly. "We're so proud of you, Jack," whispered his father.

"We might not always have been there for you," murmured his mother, "but you'll always be our son."

Caw knew what he had to say. He had to release them.

"I love you both," he said. "And . . . and I forgive you."

His parents' smiles lost their sadness completely, and in the space of a breath, they vanished.

Caw swallowed back his tears. "Good-bye," he whispered to the empty nest.

As he climbed down the tree, he noticed that the air was cooler than before and the sky was darkening into twilight. But that wasn't all that had changed. Gone was the verdant green of the forest, replaced with the hues of autumn—oranges, burnt scarlet, browns. The first of the leaves were falling by the time he reached the base of the tree. The seasons had turned in the space of just a few minutes.

And all the crows had gone. All except Milky. The forest felt desolate without them.

"Where are they?" said Caw.

You cannot command the crows here, said Milky. *Unless they wish to be commanded.* The old crow looked up at Caw, a little meekly.

"What's the matter?"

Milky shuffled as if he was embarrassed and looked away. *These other crows—the ones touched by death—they are my friends, crow talker. I alone stood by your parents when the Spinning Man came for them. The Land of the Dead almost claimed me. And perhaps it should have.*

Caw remembered the crow he'd seen in the dream of his parents—the one that tried to protect them and was overwhelmed by the spiders. He hadn't recognized that Milky from long ago—a Milky with black feathers. "You've been a loyal companion ever since I can remember," he said. "When all this is over—no matter how it ends—you must stay here."

Thank you, said Milky, with a tilt of his beak. *Now, are you prepared?*

Caw laid his hand against the rough bark of his tree and felt through his fingertips the spirits of his parents, now part of the Forest of the Dead. At peace.

We're proud of you, they'd said.

He wasn't going to let them down.

"I'm ready," he said. "Let's find the Spinning Man."

19

Leaves were falling rapidly from the trees as Caw pressed through the forest, and soon he was crunching through a carpet of brown. Instead of flying ahead, Milky perched on Caw's shoulder as he walked between the looming trunks. Caw didn't need the crows to guide him now. His feet seemed to know the way.

"Are you scared?" asked Caw.

Only a fool would not fear what awaits us, said Milky.

Before long the trees were completely bare, their trunks twisted, black, and diseased. Their skeletal forms reached up from the earth, clawing at the infinite starless dark of the night sky. The fallen leaves had dissolved into a murky, foul-smelling mulch that sucked at Caw's feet.

A cold wind stirred through the trees like a voiceless whisper that urged him to turn around and run, run while he still had the chance. It stroked his skin and slipped its fingers around his heart, squeezing like a chill fist. He ignored its warnings.

Caw's breath caught in his throat as he saw a figure emerge from behind two trunks. It was Jawbone, his slab-like features gray as ash and covered in scars—the remnants of his injuries in the real world. His smile was a joyless split in his tattooed face, but his eyes were the most terrible of all—tiny black dots for pupils in irises pale like frost.

Have no fear, said Milky. *He is too weak to harm you in this place.*

Caw hardened his resolve and walked right up to the dog feral. The pinpricks of Jawbone's eyes glittered. "Greetings, crow talker," he said.

"I'm looking for the Spinning Man," said Caw.

Jawbone grunted and turned, throwing out an arm to show the way. "He can't wait to meet you."

As they walked side by side, Caw sensed other presences moving through the darkness among the trees, keeping pace. He made out dim shapes and felt the hatred of their stares.

Disciples of the Spinning Man, said Milky. *Those who died in the Dark Summer.*

"You look scared, boy," said Jawbone. "What kind of feral are you with only one crow to protect you?"

"One more than you have dogs," said Caw.

Jawbone's face fell. "Think you're brave coming here?" he said. "You've made a mistake, crow talker. The Spinning Man will make you wield the Crow's Beak, and finally return to the Land of the Living."

"Unless I stop him," said Caw, trying to sound sure of himself.

He'd known the risks of coming here, but hearing Jawbone's taunts made it ten times worse.

Jawbone chuckled. "You were just a baby in the Dark Summer—I was *there*. I saw so many of your kind die, caught in his webs. Each a greater feral than you. The Spinning Man shows no mercy."

"I don't expect any," said Caw. "I've come to get my friend."

"The fox talker's brat?" said Jawbone. "Oh, she's quickly become quite a favorite of my master. He'll not release her."

"Then I will fight him," said Caw.

"And we'll watch," said Jawbone. "I hope the shades of your parents are listening when your screams fill this land."

Caw saw a dim light ahead between the trees.

"We're here," said Jawbone, his face full of awe. He stopped in his tracks, and Caw walked on alone.

The trees fell away on either side to reveal a clearing in the forest. Light was coming from an elaborate network of thick, luminous strands stretching from the surrounding branches. They joined in the center to form a throne of web.

Caw planted his legs and willed them not to tremble. In the seat of silken threads was the man from his nightmare, swathed from neck to feet in a black robe wrapped tightly over his body. Only the skin of his hands and face was showing, white and stretched so tightly over his skeleton that Caw could see every knotted joint of his long fingers and each jutting bone of his face. His black nails were like talons, and on one finger he wore the bulky gold ring engraved with the spider symbol. In his other hand he clutched the Crow's Beak like a scepter. He was older than in the dream, and scars crossed his face where Caw remembered it being smooth. There were streaks of white in the otherwise black sweep of his hair. In this world of shades, he looked more solid and real than anything around him.

"Hello, *Jack*," said the Spinning Man. His voice was soft and rasping. "I've been expecting you."

"Where's Lydia?" said Caw. Fear and anger threatened to overwhelm him, but his words were firm.

"Patience," said the Spinning Man. "I have waited eight long years for this. Eight years in this place, with only these sad, pathetic shadows for company, gathering the strength for my return. You must have felt it, even in the Land of the Living. Jawbone did. So did Mamba and Scuttle. I wonder, Caw, did you dream of me?"

"You'll be here till you fade to nothing!" said Caw. "Where is my friend?"

The Spinning Man smiled. Gone was the dazzling white grin from Caw's dream—his teeth were black and filed to points.

"So much like your mother," he said. "And yet even she was choking with fear when she died."

"Shut up!" said Caw. "Don't talk about my mother!"

The Spinning Man waved a long hand dismissively. "You're

right, Jack. The past is the past. It's the future that matters now. Let's get to the matter at hand, shall we?"

He reached for a strand of webbing and plucked it. The silk trembled along its length, and Caw's eyes followed. Where it met a branch there hung a spun cocoon of white stickiness. Caw gasped in horror as he made out the shadow of a body trapped within. Lydia's face was only just visible through a thin layer of silk—her eyes were open and full of fear. "Lydia!" shouted Caw.

The web coffin quivered as she struggled.

"Quite a gift," said the Spinning Man. "The daughter of the one who sent me to this place. My spiders can make her suffer so much." He smiled wickedly. "Even in the Land of the Dead, there can always be suffering."

"Let her go!" said Caw.

"Of course," said the Spinning Man. He leaned forward on his throne and whispered, "On one condition." Caw knew what it would be before the Spinning Man spoke the words. "Return me to the Land of the Living."

"Never," said Caw.

"You sound very sure," said the Spinning Man. "What if I persuade you?"

Caw heard a chattering sound and glanced sideways. The forest floor at the edge of the clearing was *moving*. He shuddered as he realized what he was looking at. Spiders—white ones of every size and shape—scurrying toward him, closing in. Others hopped up onto the strands of webbing and crawled toward Lydia.

"You have two choices, Jack Carmichael. Either cut the veil and take us back to the Land of the Living—you, me, and the girl. Or stay here, where both of you will know only agony for all eternity."

Spiders swarmed over Lydia's cocoon.

"I've waited for eight years," said the Spinning Man, as a spider walked across the exposed skin of Lydia's face. "I am stronger now than ever, and I won't wait any longer."

Caw focused on his friend, trying to keep his eyes off the pale face of the Spinning Man. What would his mother have done? She had given her life in order to save Caw's. But would she allow Lydia to be tortured in order to save the Land of the Living? Or would she take her chances and let the Spinning Man return?

Caw thought about Mrs. Strickham, Crumb and Pip, and Felix Quaker. He thought of the few ferals who'd come to listen to his pleas for help, only to walk away. They wouldn't stand a chance against the Spinning Man. The dark times would happen all over again. Blood would flow into the Blackwater and stain the streets. Blackstone would perish in the onslaught.

He glanced at Lydia. Perhaps that price was worth paying. She didn't deserve any of this.

But maybe there was another way. An idea had sparked in his mind, and he struggled to keep his eyes from betraying it.

"I'll do it," he said quietly.

Caw, no! said Milky.

The Spinning Man smiled and lowered the Crow's Beak to the ground. He rested it gently on the backs of the spiders, who carried it toward Caw's feet. Caw stooped to pick it up. The blade was light in his hand.

If you cut the veil, all is lost, said Milky. *The Spinning Man will bring a rule of terror to the Land of the Living.*

"Cross me now," said the Spinning Man, "and your friend will feel my spiders' fangs in a heartbeat. She will suffer pain beyond imagining, and you will watch."

"I'm sorry, Milky," said Caw. "I have no choice."

"Do it!" said the Spinning Man.

Caw closed his eyes and spoke to Milky with his mind instead of his voice. *You said I can't control the crows here, but they'll listen to you. I need them now.*

Caw felt a slight pressure on his shoulder as Milky took flight. Without a word of farewell, the crow receded into the darkness between the trees.

"Ha!" said the Spinning Man. "Even your oldest friend has forsaken you. Now, *cut the veil.*"

Caw lifted the Crow's Beak, and its power surged along his arm. He sensed the fabric that separated the lands drawn to its blade as he looked up at Lydia. She was shaking her head, a spider poised beside her cheek. Caw's eyes followed the thread that linked her with the throne. His grip tightened over the hilt, and his heart beat faster.

Springing into the air, he jumped sideways and brought the blade down on the silk strand, severing it with a single blow.

"No!" growled the Spinning Man, his eyes widening in shock. Before he could move, his throne, carefully balanced by the webbing, collapsed on itself, covering him in a tangle of threads. At the same time, Lydia's cocoon plummeted, thumping into the ground and throwing spiders in all directions. Caw ran to her, trampling the brittle bodies. He tore at the webbing around her face, then tugged more from her upper body.

"Caw! Look out!" she cried.

He turned as spiders surged up his body and over his arm. They started biting, making him jerk and cry out. The Crow's Beak tumbled from his hand.

"I warned you!" screamed the Spinning Man, rising to his feet.

Caw flailed as spiders covered his ankles and legs. It was his nightmare come true—the fate of his parents—and every time the spiders' fangs stabbed into his skin, he could feel the poison surging into his blood.

The clearing spun around him. He caught flashes of Lydia's face, the Spinning Man, trees at strange angles. He fell to the ground, and Lydia's screams filled his head, mixing with his own desperate cries. It was more horrible than anything he could have dreamed. He felt spiders in his hair, spiders trying to crawl into his mouth, his nostrils, and his ears. He tried to brush them away, but as soon as he did, more covered him. He was growing weaker by the second. They were trying to push open his clenched eyes, and he knew he couldn't stop them for long. A white blur filled his vision.

Then something brushed his skin.

It was a feather.

Then another.

"What?" shouted the Spinning Man.

Caw began to feel soft thumps all across his body. The screeching that followed was the most wonderful thing he'd ever heard. The cries of the crows.

He opened his eyes and saw nothing but white feathered shapes flapping over his body, and darting beaks as crows snapped up the spiders, tearing them apart and throwing them aside. He managed to stand and staggered sideways, only to be caught by Lydia. Thick strands of silk still hung from her body, but she was free. The crows formed a circle around the pair of them, pecking at any spiders that came too close.

The Spinning Man stood across the clearing. "Not bad," he said, "for a beginner. But can you do this?"

A fork of lightning split the sky above, followed by thunder so loud it shook the trees. Branches split open with whip cracks as the

Spinning Man fell to his knees, howling. Under his dark robes his body buckled. Caw felt Lydia grip his arm and pull him back. "We have to run!" she said. "Where's the Crow's Beak?"

But Caw couldn't drag his eyes from the horrible sight before him. The Spinning Man's arms and legs were stretching under his clothes, becoming thinner still. Black veins broke out under his pale skin, then seemed to burst, spreading inkiness across his flesh. A fine black fur sprouted from his fingers as they fused together into paddle-like feet. The bones of his body were grinding together and snapping jerkily into new configurations. His waist narrowed as his torso swelled.

Across his back and sides, his robe tore open as four more legs emerged on either side of his spine, snaking out and reaching toward the ground. As they touched the forest floor, the Spinning Man's head turned upward. His face grew larger, elongating as the bones of his skull shifted. His hair fell in clumps around his front legs as his jaws stretched wide. Two of his teeth jutted into dripping fangs, and then his cheeks split open to reveal two more eyes, then four, then six. As the transformation ceased, eight black orbs swiveled to rest on Caw from the dark fur of a spider's head. A giant spider that loomed as tall as Caw himself.

Lydia was scrambling through a mass of webbing on the ground. "It's got to be here somewhere!" she said.

"What do you think, crow talker?" said the huge spider in the voice of the Spinning Man.

Before Caw could answer, a flood of spiders appeared behind the giant form of their master. They poured across the clearing, overwhelming the crows. The birds thrashed and cried out in pain.

Run, Caw! shrieked Milky from somewhere beneath the mess of flapping feathers.

Caw turned and seized Lydia's hand. "Wait!" she cried. "What about the Crow's Beak?"

He yanked her after him, sprinting for the edge of the clearing. He wasn't sure where he was running to, only that to stay in the clearing with that *thing* would be a terrible mistake. As they plunged between the trees, shadows moved out of their path. He felt cold twinges as he brushed past the dead. Their voices pursued him. *Run, mortal! He follows!*

Caw glanced back and saw that they were right. The giant spider's feet thumped into the ground, and then it crashed into a tree, shaking the trunk as it pushed past. Its mandibles squirmed.

"You cannot escape me," said the spider.

Caw's feet flew over the ground in long strides, Lydia following close behind. There was nothing ahead but decayed trees, an endless gloomy forest.

"We should split up!" said Lydia, ripping her hand free of his grasp. She darted left. Caw ran straight ahead, and the breath tearing up from his lungs was sour, laced with fear. He looked around for his crows, but the dead branches above were empty. When he looked for Lydia again, she too had vanished.

He stumbled over a root, almost fell, but righted himself. He slid behind a tree trunk, back pressed against the bark, and tried to remain still.

The voice of the Spinning Man sounded distant when it broke the silence.

"This is my realm, Jack," he said. "I bend it to my will. There is no point running, because all routes lead to me."

Caw held his breath, but his heart thumped painfully in his chest.

"I can smell your fear, boy," said the Spinning Man, closer now.

Caw wondered if he should make a run for it. The farther he led the Spinning Man from the clearing, the more time he'd be able to buy Lydia. But he felt paralyzed, as though his feet had put down roots like the trees around him. A long shadow moved to his left, and from the way it arced, he knew it was a spider leg. Then the bristling limb appeared, just a few feet away, treading lightly. The air was cold. He forced his body to move and ran.

"There you are!" hissed the voice.

Caw's feet seemed to snag, and he tumbled to the ground. His face hit the mud, and some forced its way into his mouth. Caw squirmed onto his back and realized his legs were stuck together by some sort of slime. Terror made him breathless. It was webbing.

The Spinning Man squeezed his arachnid bulk between the trees.

"You're going nowhere, crow talker."

Caw tore the webbing with grime-covered hands and managed to free one foot. He staggered upright, but the giant black spider arched his back and a fresh strand of silk shot out from a spike at the base of his abdomen. The sticky substance looped around Caw's ankles and yanked him onto the ground again.

He felt his body dragged across the earth, as the Spinning Man brought him toward the clearing. Sharp roots dug into his back, but the spider pulled him effortlessly along. Caw rolled over and tried to slow himself with his hands, but there was nothing to hold on to. His ribs thumped into a tree, and he gasped in pain. He raised his arms to ward off another blow and managed to grip a trunk, trying to tug himself free. He felt his nails catch on the bark, then a lancing agony as one of them tore away.

He slid helplessly into the middle of the clearing, where the white crows were still struggling against the onslaught of spiders. As the Spinning Man's shadow fell over him, Caw rolled and saw the deformed, mottled face of his enemy inches from his own. Two legs stabbed into the ground on either side of his head, and the black portions of the spider's body heaved.

He tried to breathe, tried to stay calm. He closed his eyes, knowing he might never get another chance. He wasn't ready for the end.

"Let him go!" yelled Lydia. "I have the Crow's Beak."

Caw twisted his neck and saw Lydia standing nearby. In her hand was the sword.

Why had she come back? Why couldn't she have run? He had to do *something*. The power built suddenly inside Caw, like floodwater behind a dam. He felt a wind within him rise and flutter the tips of his ragged jacket. He released it, throwing out his summons. He felt its reach spread across the clearing and beyond. It sought every crow in the forest.

The Spinning Man laughed, and Caw felt spools of white fluid trickle onto his neck.

"The time for bargains is over, little girl," said the spider. "I'll get what I want in the end, but first he has to pay for his insolence. By the time I've finished, he'll be begging for me to let him use the Crow's Beak. And don't worry, child—it's your turn next!"

Come to me! Caw screamed with his mind. *Please! I need you.* The strength of his feral spirit clutched each of the crows in its talons. They gave themselves to him, and he felt the power of their beating wings and the anger of their stabbing beaks, threatening almost to overwhelm him. But the power was his. His consciousness seemed to burst free of the tethers in his mind. He became the crows and they became him. He saw the dark forest under the collective span of his wings, he saw the clearing and the eight-legged form lurking at its center.

"Ready to suffer?" said the Spinning Man.

Caw opened his eyes to see the Spinning Man's jaws gaping wide above his face.

Beyond, a thousand crows made the sky white.

"Now!" said Caw.

The sky fell as one.

20

The Spinning Man's eight eyes went wide as the crows slammed into his legs and back. One must have severed the thread holding Caw, because suddenly his ankles were free. He rolled out from beneath the black abdomen as the spider's legs buckled. Still the crows came, sinking their talons and beaks into the leathered shell. Caw's anger drove them on, and each time one thumped into the spider's body, it felt like he was smashing the Spinning Man with his own fists.

A mixture of animal grunting and wild cries echoed across the clearing. A foul stench filled the air as the spider's body disintegrated before Caw's eyes. The legs were first to go, pecked to nothing, and then the abdomen gave way, collapsing in on itself. A black liquid like spilled oil pooled beneath the spider's broken skull. Caw stepped back, and for a split second he thought he saw the writhing, thin shape of the Spinning Man, all pale skin and torn clothes. Lydia was at his side, wincing in disgust.

The crows' fervor seemed to dim, their attack less frantic, and Caw lifted his hand. The birds obeyed, taking flight into the surrounding trees, their wings stained black from the spider's gore.

Nothing remained on the ground except a glinting golden ring. Caw gazed at it in wonder, unable to believe that it was the last remaining piece of the monster he had faced. Gingerly, he crouched down to pick it up. It was as cold as ice.

Lydia joined him. "That was incredible!" she said. "How did you do that?"

Caw glanced at the crows perched around the clearing. He spotted Milky among them. "I didn't," he said. He nodded toward the birds. "They did."

"Thank you," said Lydia. "All of you!" The crows let out a chorus of soft warbles, and Lydia whispered to Caw, "But especially to you. I can't believe you came for me."

Caw smiled shyly, half wishing the moment would pass, and half wishing it would go on forever.

"It's nothing compared to what you did, jumping through that portal," Caw replied. "I knew there was a chance I could find my way home, being the crow feral and all. But you . . . you came here thinking there was no going back."

Lydia bit her lip. "It was a bit stupid, wasn't it?"

"It was amazing," Caw said. Then, with a grin, he added, "But don't do it again. Okay?"

Lydia held out the Crow's Beak. "Let's go home," she said.

Caw took the curved sword from her, then nodded to Milky. "Good-bye, Milky."

Milky cocked his head. *Farewell, crow talker.*

The pale crow took off, and one by one the rest of the flock peeled after him, leaving Caw and Lydia alone.

Caw felt completely drained, his nerves shredded, but he lifted the sword with a sense of triumph. He scythed the blade through the air, and a dark cut appeared in front of them, opening to blackness deeper than any starless night. He reached out a hand for Lydia, and she took it.

"Ready?" he said.

She nodded, and they stepped into the void together. The darkness folded around Caw with a sound like rushing water, and he felt suddenly weightless, like his soul had separated from his body. He floated along, as if in a dream, but all the while he still sensed Lydia at his side.

A thin strip of light appeared in the distance, and they hurtled toward it, faster and faster. The light became blinding, and Caw opened his mouth to scream, but no sound came out. As the radiance enveloped his whole world, Caw gave himself up to it and closed his eyes.

A shock wave passed over his body, and he felt solid ground beneath his feet. He stumbled forward and looked around, his eyes slowly adjusting to the gloom.

He was standing in the basement of the sewing factory, holding Lydia's hand.

Caw had expected to arrive in the graveyard beside his parents' resting place, but now his heart lurched. He saw not just Crumb but Mrs. Strickham too, both on their knees with their hands tied behind their backs and snakes looped around their necks. Behind them stood Scuttle and Mamba.

"Look who it is!" said the black-clad woman. "How perfect. The fox feral wasn't easy to catch, but you've just come straight to us."

"Lydia!" said Mrs. Strickham. Her coat was torn, and she looked exhausted.

"Mom!" said Lydia.

Scuttle's eyes fell on the Crow's Beak and then flicked to Caw's face. "Where is he? Where's the Spinning Man?"

"The Spinning Man is gone," said Caw. "Destroyed."

The blood drained from Scuttle's face, but Mamba's features hardened.

"You're lying!" she hissed.

Caw dug in his pocket and pulled out the golden ring.

"He's telling the truth," said Lydia, "so you might as well give up."

Scuttle stared at the ring, his eyes burning with fury. "Or we could kill you all," he said. He twitched his head and suddenly a cockroach raced up Caw's leg, down his arm, and onto his hand and bit deep into his flesh. Caw cried out in pain, the ring dropping and skittering across the floor into the shadows. He shook off the roach, only to see an army of its brethren emerging from the corners of the room.

Mamba hissed, and Lydia's mother and Crumb cried out as the snakes around their necks tightened their coils. Then Caw saw something strange. Two mice were scurrying under the door. And mice meant only one thing. . . .

Pip burst into the room, wild-eyed and panting. "Let them go!" he cried.

Scuttle sniggered and shot a glance at Mamba. "Oh, now I *am* scared."

"You should be," said Pip.

An electrical hum sounded from somewhere in the walls.

"What's that?" said Mamba, taking a step backward.

Across the ceiling, from the suspended air-conditioning vents, came a series of thumps. Something was running inside. The hum became a loud, resonating buzz. And suddenly Caw realized what was creating it.

"Get down!" he hissed.

He flattened himself to the floor, pulling Lydia down with him, as a dark cloud of bees swept through the door behind Pip and fell upon Mamba and Scuttle. They writhed and jerked, letting out panicked screams and shrieks as the insects coated their skin.

"Help me!" wailed Mamba. With their mistress distracted, the snakes fell from the necks of Crumb and Velma Strickham.

Scuttle fell to the ground and rolled over, managing to shake a few bees off. He reached for a fire extinguisher leaning against a wall and directed it at Mamba, blasting the bees off her with white foam. A wave of roaches shot across the floor in all directions, but gray shapes dropped from the ceiling, landing nimbly on the floor. Squirrels! They set about the roaches with claw and tooth, crunching their brittle shells. Caw scrambled away from the battle, leading Lydia by the hand.

Coated in white foam, Mamba was waving her arms desperately. But as her snakes surged at Caw and his friends, more squirming shapes met them on the ground. Giant centipedes tangled with the slithering army, driving them back.

"Go ferals!" cried Pip.

At the door, three figures had joined him. Madeleine in her wheelchair, her dark eyes gleaming; Ali the bee talker standing tall, with his hand resting on the shoulder of the old woman, Emily, who commanded the centipedes. "Run!" yelled Scuttle, his face and lips swollen from bee stings. He scurried toward a door Caw hadn't seen before, on the opposite side of the room. Mamba strode past him at speed, thrust the door open, and vanished. Caw's fist tightened on the Crow's Beak. He was about to give chase, when he heard Mamba scream. She reentered the room, staggering backward.

"Please! Don't hurt me. Make it go away!"

Scuttle stopped dead in his tracks, and Caw's heart lurched as he saw the huge brown wolf padding slowly into the room from the open doorway. Drool spilled from its white teeth as its lips curled. Racklen followed.

"Long time no see, Scuttle," he said. "I seem to remember we have some unfinished business."

The roach talker trembled, pressing his hands together as if in prayer. "Don't know what you mean!" he said.

The wolf growled.

"You said you'd skin Cressida here and wear her as a coat," said Racklen. "She says she'd prefer the other way around."

Caw saw Scuttle's Adam's apple bob in his throat. "A misunderstanding, I'm sure. Perhaps we could talk about it."

Emily the centipede feral hobbled slowly into the room. "The time for talking is over," she said coldly. "It's time for blood."

Her centipedes uncoiled themselves from Mamba's dead snakes and began to inch toward the bad ferals. Ali snapped his fingers, summoning a fresh column of bees from the air-conditioning vents. Madeleine's squirrels hopped onto crates, all directing their eyes toward Scuttle and Mamba. Caw had never known the little furry creatures could look so menacing.

"Wait," said Velma Strickham. She had stepped forward and put her arms around Lydia. "This isn't the way we do things."

"This is war," said Racklen. "This is revenge for what they did to us." He placed a hand in the thick hackles of his wolf, looking at

Scuttle with pure hatred. "Tear them apart, my girl," he said softly.

"No!" shouted Caw, leaping between the wolf and the Spinning Man's cowering disciples. The beast stopped a foot from him, their faces almost level. Even if his crows had been here, he knew they could do nothing for him now. "We've seen enough bloodshed," he said, trying to fight the fear that threatened to break his voice. "These ferals are at our mercy."

The wolf's yellow eyes watched him, and Caw hoped that Racklen had firm control of its instincts. With one bite it could crush his skull.

"Listen to him, wolf talker," said Crumb. "The war is over and we fought for good, remember? *They* were the ones who killed without pity."

Finally, the wolf backed away.

"You did the right thing," said Velma. "Your wife would have been proud of you, Racklen."

A sudden pounding of footsteps made everyone spin around. Light was coming from down the corridor.

"Freeze!" shouted a voice. "Police!"

"Go!" said Velma. "Get out of here!"

Ali grabbed the handles of Madeleine's wheelchair and pushed her across the room as Racklen turned, his wolf slinking past him. The wolf talker waited next to the door he'd entered by until Emily had passed through as well. Crumb and Pip were the last to leave.

Then Caw was blinded by flashlights, seeing only silhouettes of figures, some running, some crouching.

"Police! On your knees!"

Caw saw the glint of metal gun barrels.

"Drop the weapon!"

He realized they were talking to him and let the Crow's Beak fall. He got to his knees, raising his hands. Lydia had already done the same.

"It's the boy from the library!" said an officer. A moment later Caw felt his hands yanked behind his back and the chill metal of cuffs being locked into place.

"Out of the way!" Caw recognized Mr. Strickham's gruff voice. "Lydia! Velma! Get off them—that's my wife and daughter!"

"Dad!"

Caw felt himself dragged upright. He looked at the Crow's Beak desperately, but there was no way he could reach it.

"Lydia! Velma!" said Mr. Strickham. "I thought you were both— I thought— Thank God!"

Two policemen bundled Caw out of the room and up the stairs. He heard Lydia's voice from behind. "Dad, they've got Caw!" she was saying. There were more officers lining the corridor ahead. He heard someone shouting, ". . . dozens of damned foxes in here! I've never seen anything like it."

"Dad!" shouted Lydia again. "Where are they taking him? He saved me!"

Caw was half dragged, half pushed through the room full of sewing machines, then through the door and into the daylight. Four police cars and two armored vans sat at the roadside. Caw felt his cuffs being loosened on one wrist. "Stay put!" said one of the police officers, fastening the other cuff to a steel railing. His radio crackled. "Did you say *bees*?" he muttered. Caw almost smiled. The other ferals had been hiding for years—they wouldn't let themselves be caught now.

A moment later, Scuttle and Mamba came through the door, both cuffed and surrounded by officers in riot gear. The ferals were silent and pale as they were escorted to a van and pushed inside.

"Hold still and don't turn around," whispered a voice behind him.

"Pip?" said Caw.

"Shh! I'm going to try and pick the lock."

A few seconds later, the pressure vanished from Caw's wrists. He drew his hands around slowly, then turned. Pip had gone, and the cuffs dangled loose on the railing.

Mr. and Mrs. Strickham emerged from the factory doors with Lydia between them, hugging one another tightly. It made Caw's heart swell to see it.

"Officer Franco?" said Mr. Strickham. "We need to talk about the boy."

One of the cops who'd escorted Caw from the building came

running over to the warden. "We've got him, sir," he said. "Secured to that railing over—"

But Caw had already hopped over the railing and melted into the shadows between two buildings.

He couldn't go back to the nest, he knew that. It was the first place they'd look for him.

Which left only one possibility.

He woke to the smell of bacon under the eaves of the church. Crumb leaned over his brazier, moving around a battered frying pan. Pale morning light filtered through the windows and the hole in the roof.

"Morning, sleepy," he said.

Caw sat up quickly and immediately wished he hadn't. His body ached all over, from the tips of his toes to his scalp. He groaned.

"Turning into a crow will do that," said Crumb, chuckling. He handed Caw a plate with a greasy bacon sandwich and a steaming Styrofoam cup. Then he sagged to the floor opposite and sank his teeth into a sandwich of his own. "Is it true, then? Is he gone?"

Caw took an enormous bite and nodded, remembering the mad swimming eyes of the Spinning Man in his final moments.

"Long may he remain so," said Crumb. He chewed thoughtfully. "You know, Caw, you can stay here for good, if you like."

Caw smiled. "Thank you," he said, "but you don't have to say that."

Crumb shrugged. "Yes, I do," he said. He delved into one of his many pockets and took out a folded square of newspaper. He held it out to Caw.

The paper felt delicate, and Caw opened it carefully. It was a black-and-white photograph of a man and a woman. Caw recognized their faces—his mother and father. On the man's shoulders sat a boy of three or four, his legs dangling. Caw swallowed thickly, staring at the younger version of himself, before returning his gaze to his parents. They were both grinning happily.

"I thought you should have this," said Crumb.

Caw managed to speak at last. "Where's it from?"

"Quaker," he said. "He gave it to me last night. It's from a story printed after they died. I know what it's like to lose your parents, Caw. So putting you up—it's the least I can do."

Caw folded the paper again and slipped it into his coat. "Thank you," he said.

He sat up straighter at the sound of footsteps on the stairs, but Crumb just kept munching on his sandwich. "Hello, Pip!" the pigeon talker called.

The blond-haired boy edged into the room. "Found a couple of friends of yours, Caw," he said, nodding to the broken stained-glass window at the far end of the nave. Glum and Screech flew in, tilting back their wings as they landed beside Caw.

Where'd you go? asked Glum. *We waited at the graveyard for hours!*

"It's a long story," said Caw.

First things first—is that bacon? asked Screech.

Caw tore off a bit and threw it to the crow, who caught it and snapped it up in his beak.

"And guess what?" said Pip. "I've got something else of yours." He lifted a filthy blanket from beside the brazier and carefully unwrapped it. Lying inside was a long, gleaming black blade—the Crow's Beak.

"Nicked it from a snoozing cop," said Pip. "So, Caw," he added shyly. "Are you going to stay here with us?"

Caw sipped his drink and tasted hot chocolate. Miss Wallace's face sprang up in his mind, and he felt a wave of sorrow. He looked at Pip's expectant face.

"I don't know," he said. "I think—I think I need to be on my own for a while."

"Of course," said Crumb. "Is there anything you need?"

Caw was about to say no, but then a thought occurred to him.

"There is one thing," he said.

That afternoon, Caw took a bus for the first time in his life, dressed in clothes borrowed from Crumb. He'd wound a scarf up around his face and pulled a baseball cap as low as he could in case anyone recognized him from the newspapers. For once, his crows agreed to stay behind. They knew this was something Caw needed to do alone.

The wheezing bus took him out of Blackstone to a small village beyond called Falston. There he disembarked and walked through the gate of the churchyard and up the path between the graves. He took a single battered white rose from his pocket and placed it beside his parents' headstone, then ran his fingers around the loops and lines of their names. One day, perhaps, he would be able to read them.

Caw drew the photograph from his jacket and smoothed it out against the marble.

Could Crumb ever replace them? Of course he couldn't. But he would be a companion, sort of like an older brother, and Caw didn't doubt that the pigeon feral could teach him a thing or two about survival in Blackstone. He wasn't sure how Screech and Glum would take to living alongside the pigeons, but he guessed they'd learn to cope. Crows were survivors, as Glum often said.

Or perhaps he could build himself a new nest, somewhere safer than the park. With a hundred crows working for him, it would take only a fraction of the time. Something told him he wouldn't, though. He'd lived alone for so long already. Maybe it was time for some human company.

"I thought you might be here," said Lydia.

Caw almost dropped the photo and stood quickly. She was standing a few yards away, wrapped up warmly in a thick green coat, with a green hat and scarf, and her hands tucked in her pockets.

"How did you find me?" he said.

Lydia smiled, withdrew a gloved hand, and pointed across the churchyard. Caw saw Mrs. Strickham sitting in the driver's seat of their car. She waved.

"My mom knew where your parents were buried," she said. "Her foxes have sharp eyes, apparently." She looked at the grave. "Carmichael—it's a nice name."

Caw held out the picture to her. "That's them—my parents," he said proudly.

"They look kind," Lydia said. She frowned. "Is that you? You were cute!"

Caw blushed.

Lydia laughed, then looked suddenly serious. "How come you left without saying good-bye last night?"

"Sorry," said Caw. "I had to. Is that why you came here—to say good-bye?"

Lydia threw a quick glance at her mother. "No," she said. "I came to ask if you wanted to live with us—for a while at least."

"But—"

"Hear me out," she said. "We've got a spare room. My dad says it's okay. We won't tell him about you being a feral, of course. He doesn't even know about Mom! Your table manners need a bit of work, sure, and a couple of days in the bathroom wouldn't hurt. Then there's your wardrobe, which frankly—"

"Okay, okay," said Caw, holding up a hand. "I get the idea."

"So you'll come?" said Lydia, her face lighting up.

Caw hesitated. A real home, with a real bed and a real family and real meals eaten around a table . . . "I'll have to talk to the crows, but . . ." He paused as he spotted something in her hair—a piece of fluff—and reached out to brush it away.

His hand jerked back as the piece of fluff dropped to the ground and scrambled away on eight legs. His blood ran cold.

"What is it?" said Lydia, snapping her head around.

"Nothing," Caw said quickly. "Just a moth."

But it wasn't nothing. It was a spider. A spider white as bone.

"So you were saying you'll clear it with the crows, right? I'm sure they'll love having a bit more nest space. Or they could build a new nest in the garden!"

The spider. It might mean nothing. The Spinning Man *was* dead, wasn't he? But if he wasn't . . .

"I can't," he said suddenly. "I'm sorry. I think my place is with Crumb for now. And you're right, my table manners . . ."

"I was joking!" said Lydia.

"I know," said Caw, "but I'm serious. I don't think I'm ready yet. Not for that sort of life."

Lydia's face fell. "If that's how you feel," she said. "But the offer's always open."

"And I'm grateful," said Caw. "Honestly."

A car horn sounded down the hill, and Lydia looked toward her mother. "I've got to go," she said. She leaned forward and hugged Caw tight. He felt another rush of blood to his face as Lydia backed away slowly down the path. "Good-bye, Jack Carmichael," she said. "For now at least. Remember I promised to teach you to read. You're not getting out of it!"

Caw grinned and glanced at his parents' grave, waiting for the blush to subside.

Elizabeth and Richard Carmichael. Two names that didn't tell half the story.

He'd had no idea what his real name was until Felix Quaker told him. He hadn't been called Jack since he was five years old, and he wasn't about to start now.

He called down the graveyard to Lydia as she opened the car door. "My name isn't Jack," he said. "It's Caw."

Lydia smiled. "Bye then, Caw!" she called back, waving.

Caw, the crow talker. Caw, last descendant of a line going back hundreds of years. What would the following days bring?

He took a deep breath of the frigid air and felt it cleanse him.

Somehow he knew the threat wasn't gone for good. There were other ferals out there—bad as well as good. One enemy was defeated, but more would come.

And Caw would be ready.